The Document Matters

Also by Brandon Daily:

A Murder Country
The Valley

Praise for
Darkening

"From the hardscrabble lives of the present age, to questions of the near future, to the gray ghosts of the war-torn past—Daily handles them all with taught evocative language that reminds of Michael Farris Smith and Ron Rash. The range here is remarkable and the stories ring with truth and beauty."

—Christian Kiefer,
author of *The Animals* and *Phantoms*

"*Darkening* is an impressionistic fever dream. Daily conjures a remarkably dark vision, one where we'd be doomed if it weren't for the faintest glint of light off in the distance, one we still recognize as hope."

—Jarret Middleton,
author of *Darkansas*

"A rich exploration of the macabre, the sinister, and the fantastic, Brandon Daily's *Darkening* deftly navigates the strange and sublime territory of the human psyche through genres ranging from science fiction to horror to realism. This book will leave you delightfully disturbed."

—Lindsey Drager,
author of *The Lost Daughter Collective*
and *The Archive of Alternate Endings*

"In this deeply imagined book, Brandon Daily turns toward the shadows to introduce us to the underappreciated and overlooked with lyric noir energy. As I tunneled along with characters in their harshest moments, these gripping, tough stories compelled me to consider my capacity for understanding the strange and the disturbing—ultimately demonstrating page after page how hope dwells equally in both darkness and shafts of light."

—Melissa Fraterrigo,
author of *Glory Days*

ABC Group Documentation //
878 Mallory Drive
Marietta, GA 30062

Interior design by J David Osborne

Grateful acknoweldgment is made by the author to the editors of the following publications, where these stories first appeared.

"Darkening" appeared in *RiverLit Magazine,* 2012. "Stormdance" appeared in *Phoebe: A Journal of Literature,* 2014. "One Last Time" appeared in *Prick of the Spindle Magazine,* 2014. "Avenues" will appear in *Shotgun Honey Presents: Volume 4,* forthcoming. "In the Woods" appeared in *Flash Fiction Magazine,* 2018. "A Lovely" appeared in *Prick of the Spindle Magazine,* 2012. "South of Salvation" appeared in *Prick of the Spindle Magazine,* 2012, and was the winner of the CAST Players National One-Act Playwriting Competition—Performed 2012.

ISBN: 978-1-64396-068-5

Printed in the USA.

Darkening:

stories and a novella

by

Brandon Daily

For Sawyer and Elliette,
There is always light in the darkness

CONTENTS

When we are born, we cry that we are come
To this great stage of fools.

—William Shakespeare, *King Lear*

The miserable have no other medicine but only hope.

—William Shakespeare, *Measure for Measure*

Darkening

And he lays flat during the day, digging the back of his skull into the wooden bottom of the boat, afraid to sit up and be seen, afraid they might shoot at him, or bring him in and take him back. He's still unsure which would be worse.

At night, he sits up and stretches his back and holds the oars and begins to gently move them through the water. Ripples form around the wood of them, moving off toward the shore but never fully making the distance. He hears the fish pass below him. At times, water laps over the rim of the boat and a spray hits his face, cold and then warm. He cups handfuls of water from the river and brings them to his mouth—it smells sour but tastes sweet on his tongue and he smiles. The night is cold and he wraps the blanket around his body. He'll sometimes look out into the darkness, out to the empty banks of the river to where he hears animals move quickly through the bushes and trees. Birds fly above him, but nothing else. He feels alone.

He tries to sleep as much as he can during the day, but the sun hurts his eyes and he cannot. He feels a man now, not a child or the youth he once saw when he would see his reflection. He is a man now, but, in that, he is no longer innocent of guilt or capable of forgiveness. And he is not without worry. Rather, he feels a man capable of being and surviving, and his memories remind him of this.

* * *

Her face appears as a dream: warm and webbed, a counter against the night. He cries when he remembers. He tries to forget, but he cannot. There is no forgetting and he understands this. He tries to reach out, across the space of the boat, to where her face hovers in the night. He wants to touch it, but her face is too far away and all he can feel is the air as it slips through his fingers like the dirt that once stained his face and hands and blinded his eyes. She is invisible and without form now. On some nights, he tries to speak to her: "I know you don't exist here," he whispers, "but I wish you did and I wish you could tell me it will be all right." He continues to move the oars through the dark waters.

When he closes his eyes, he sometimes will see the candle in the blackened room. It moves freely, shifting of its own choice, bending so gently and smoothly that it seems on a string, pulled here and there, caressed and sent back to its origin without loss or change of form. The light laps against her face; her smile calm and sad. He reaches out in the night, caressing her arms, the sweat sticking to her skin. It is warm. When he opens his eyes, he sees his hands gently sliding along the wooden rim of the boat and he lets go and listens to his breath as it escapes into the night, and he shudders and lies back again, letting the moon's outline steady his thoughts. Soon he will close his eyes again and dream and it will be of her.

"I can get you out of this place," he said to her. The shed was dusty and smelled of rotten flowers and old vegetables, sulfur and sweat. "We can escape from here."

She nodded slightly and then moved her face toward his and kissed him gently on his neck. "There's no point to try," she said. The flame between them swayed back and forth, delicately moving toward each of their bodies. She picked the candle up, letting the flame hover in the air, and he could see her face in quiet shadows and the tears running down her cheeks and the sad smile just before she blew the flame out and the room was cast in darkness again and all that was left was the sound of each other's breath and the feel of each other's skin. And he whispered slowly, "There's always a point to try."

He can hear the screams in the wind when it blows at night. He sits up, his eyes open. He remains alert, looking around him. Sometimes he smells it too, and when that happens the memories return and he is left hopeless, and he weeps. He imagines the flakes floating around him now as they had then. His eyes sting and he blinks them violently and his skin feels as though hundreds of ants are crawling on it. He scratches at his arms and his legs and he begins to cry. He takes his jacket off and looks at it and begins to tear the emblem off it. His hands shake and his fingers begin to bleed as his nails dig the stitching from the material and finally he is left holding the patch. He looks at it again, studying it, and in the darkening of the night, just before the sun's rise, he can see the cold blackness of the emblem. He lets it fall into the water and float on as it may, and he puts the jacket on again.

He saw the others standing close together next to the shed, their guns slung over their shoulders. He could hear the screams from inside the shed and laughter from the others as they waited their turn. He turned to go but looked back at them, a sickness inside his body swelling. In the distance, he could see the tops of the funneled smokestacks, the constant spew of flakes and the smell of burning flesh and rot that drifted down everywhere. The ground was stained a charcoaled white from the ash. *Hell's snow*, he thought. And he knew then, as the flakes drifted around him, landing on his hands and face and in his eyes, as the screams echoed in his mind and the sickness hardened inside his stomach, he knew then that he needed to leave and he needed to take her with him.

He draws the blanket over his body and he shivers in the cold of the night. He can hear her voice whispering quietly as it sounded the first day he met her so many years before, when they were both children and he believed all people to be the same. That memory seems like a cracked photograph now, where he can all but make out the edges of the people and of the place, but those people and that place do not exist anymore.

"Shhh," she whispered. "I'll meet you on the shore where we first met. I'll wait for you forever if I have to." He looked at her face and remembered that first day he saw her: her hair stretched down her back, and the embarrassed smile she gave as he handed her the flower he picked from the river's edge, and the excitement he felt as they walked, holding hands, back up to the road where each of their houses were. He saw that girl in the woman standing before him, the woman whose eyes looked stained with tears. Her body fragile and weak now, her head shaved. He felt that girl in the tender touch of her hands and the sadness of her smile. And, in that moment, he loved her more than ever before.

His body aches from the days spent adrift on the water. He dreams of reaching the shore, of the heavy jolt as the boat runs aground and he looks to the bank and sees her waiting for him, her hair long again and stretching down her back, her face bright and a smile on her lips. He knows it to be a lie, but he believes it. He believes that she was able to escape as she promised. He believes that she was right when she told him to go on without her, that it would be easier for him to leave alone, that an officer walking a prisoner out of the camp would be cause for alarm. He believes that the hole he dug on the eastern end of the camp wasn't filled in, that she was able to find it and that she was able to crawl through it and leave. He believes that he will soon be able to embrace her and they will escape to some place where there is only truth and freedom and love. But there is so much doubt.

He breathes deep and listens to the sounds of the world around him as he feels the boat float on effortlessly, as if propelled by some unseen hand on his maker's altar. And he smiles as he closes his eyes and sees his life before him and the memories that she will make with him after he finds her again; and he hopes that it will be just so. And he hopes, because that is all that is left for him now.

Riverrun

Janine called last night.

It's been over twenty years since I've talked to her. I can't even begin to count the times in those twenty years that I've picked up the phone and dialed her number—all except that last digit. Throughout the years, Mom still talked to hers, and she would give me Janine's new number every few years, when Janine and Kyle moved each time. Six years ago, or so, Kyle got sick and died; from that point on Janine's number stayed the same.

Those nights, I'd dial and remain frozen to the spot, my finger hovering centimeters above that last button, sometimes even resting my finger on the plastic of it, feeling the slight give of it underneath. I'd hear my breath through the earpiece, like some endless circle of sound. I'd wonder if I breathed hard enough into the phone would I be able to hear the sound of my soul, like how a conch shell speaks the ocean's words.

In those moments of hesitation, I'd think of the inevitable second after the ring when I'd hear the static pick-up on the other side of the country or world, wherever she was—Mom only gave me the phone number, never the address. I had no idea what I'd say in that moment after Janine said "Hello." That's why I would hang up every time. What could I say? "Remember when we were young and thought life was going to be perfect, when we were just two little girls and things seemed so easy. When you were named Janie and I was Susie, and I'd fishtail your hair and you'd make sloppy braids of mine? Remember how we searched for treasure in the woods and came to the river that summer morning and lost ourselves there for the whole of our lives?"

I think the question I really wanted to ask but never could was whether it was all real. Was he real or did we just make-believe him up, just like we did when we were five and six and played tea party with the teddy bears in my parents' loft upstairs?

I could never find the right words, and so I gave up trying.

Janine found those words, though, last night. She found the words I never could say out loud, and they began with a simple *Hey. It's me.* And I had to sit down on the couch so as not to drop the phone from surprise. Or maybe it was joy, I don't know.

From where we stood on the river's bank that morning, we could only see the red and blue of his jacket. At first it seemed a mirage over the upstream water, some trick the early sun was playing on our eyes. Or a bird set down on a branch floating on the river. I remember how I hid myself behind a tree, how the cool of the bark felt against my cheek. Janie was next to me, her body warm against my bare arm. Her hand reached out and held onto mine, and I could feel the sweat on her palm from the walk and from the moment.

I turned to ask Janie what we should do, but her head was down and I could see her shoulders shaking from either fear or the cold of the air, I never knew which, and I never asked. Instead, I tightened my hold on her hand and looked back to the river, waiting for some movement from the jacket and the body that I knew was inside of it. Some indication of life that did not come, try as I might to will it on.

My parents' house lay on the edge of the woods. From the house, the river was only a half-mile or so away. A dusty and hidden path cut winding through the dark pines and maples and hemlocks and dogwoods and led straight to the water.

It had been the first morning of summer break. The night before, we'd celebrated moving on from seventh grade to eighth. We were in my parents' yard and I remember the sound of Janie's voice, how it dropped low, like she was telling a ghost story. "Timmy

Russel said it's out there in the woods. Said it the other day. Said he and his daddy were gonna set out and find it."

"What?" I asked.

"Gold treasure," she said. "Said his daddy found a piece big as his palm out there."

"Just a story, like all the others he tells," I said. We'd known Timmy since the kindergarten. He was a lanky kid with scruffy hair that covered his eyes most of the time, try as he might to shake it away with quick jerks of his head. Timmy took joy in stories of fantasy, telling them each with the straight face of seriousness. He never smiled. His front three teeth—top two and one lower—had been knocked out by his dog a year or two earlier. We all knew the family was poor and couldn't afford to fix his teeth. His mom worked a night job in one of the factories in Barrett while his dad worked one job on weekdays and another on weekends. But Timmy's sister was sick with cancer, Mom said once, and that's where all their money went. Mom said Timmy told stories to escape his life, if even for a minute. Said everyone told some type of story in their life to escape the things they didn't want to admit were real.

"But this one's true, not like the other one," Janie said. I knew she was talking about the story Timmy had told about his grandpa a year earlier. He'd said that his grandpa was in the Navy and had been captured by Russians on a submarine in the middle of the Atlantic Ocean. A few weeks later, we came to learn that Timmy never even knew his grandpa, that he'd been dead since before Timmy was born. "This one is true, though," Janie repeated. "I know it, and I'm goin out first thing tomorrow morning."

I couldn't tell how long we stayed hidden behind that tree, watching the water's flow around the jacket before we moved slowly down to the water's edge and then up toward where he floated. As we got closer, we could see that his right foot had been wedged and caught in a log fallen centuries ago, its bark crumbled in places, fine, like powder.

He seemed to move on his own—his arms swaying above his head, his legs kicking at the water that swirled past him—though we knew that it was just the water moving him. Leaves and small branches coasted downstream, some becoming trapped in his underside and staying there to rest for several seconds before breaking free and drifting beyond us.

Without thought or hesitation, Janie waded out into the cold river water. Her body moved slowly and I wondered as I watched her whether time itself had slowed as she walked over to him. She reached out and grabbed hold of the jacket, tugging at him until he broke free from the log; she was able to bring him to her in a bear hug. I moved down to the two of them and helped her to bring him up to the riverbank.

Janie was breathing hard when we set him down. His face was still hidden from us. An empty knot had formed in my stomach and I thought that I could grab hold of it through my skin and wrench it free if I tried, but my body couldn't move. Several seconds passed and Janie's breath slowed so I could no longer hear it. Above us, a falcon set down on a tree branch and broke the silence of the moment. I suddenly could hear the water behind me, a woodpecker's knocking somewhere deep within the woods, the rustle of ground squirrels and other animals along the pine-littered floors. I smiled as I looked around, hearing and seeing the world for the first time, it seemed.

When I looked back to the boy at my feet, I saw Janie bent down and unzipping his jacket. She touched her nose to his. "Help me," she said, looking up at me. Her face was wet. I couldn't tell if it was river water or tears. A quiet smile spread across her face, as if she knew something I was still not aware of. "He's beautiful," she said. "He's ours."

And, so, I knelt down and helped her.

We were so little then, Janine said on the phone last night. *I found some pictures the other day in my mom's house—she died last week.* I said I didn't know and that I was sorry to hear about it. *Thanks,* she said. *In one of the boxes were all the old polaroids of us then. In one of them you were wearing those overalls you always wore. I was leaning against my bike. You remember it? The blue and purple one I got that one Christmas. God, I can remember us riding up and down the street on that thing. Pedaling as fast as we could, our clothes flapping in the wind.* I told her I remembered it.

* * *

That first week after we found him, we arranged him in different positions; sometimes he would lay against a rock, his hands cupped behind his head in relaxation, while other times he'd sit cross-legged with the two of us on either side of him. That first day, we stripped him naked (it was the first time either of us had seen a penis, and we tried not to stare for fear of making him feel uncomfortable). We dried his clothes in the sun on one of the large boulder-rocks along the side of the river. After an hour, the clothes were dried and we stubbornly dressed him, talking him through each action we were about to perform: *I'm just gonna slip your arm in here. Just like that. There you go.*

Those days along the river were always quiet, the sound of nature the only voice we heard besides our own.

His skin was a light blue and always felt so cold under our hands. We'd rub our palms over his face and his arms to try and warm him. I remember one morning when I slowly moved my hand over to his, interlocking our fingers together in a loose webwork of white and blue skin. I felt a lightness in my stomach then, something I'd never felt before and haven't felt since. Janie was sitting there next to us, looking out over the quiet river, but when she looked over at me I quickly let go of his hand. I didn't want her to see.

Janie would often ask him who he was, his name. *What happened to you?* She'd place her hand on his arm and gently run her fingertips up and down his skin. She'd ask and we'd wait, and then she would rephrase the question. I stayed quiet during those moments, just watching the two of them.

One afternoon, I broke the silence of the riverbank and spoke aloud to him. "What's your name?" I said. Both Janie and I waited for several seconds, longer than when Janie asked her questions, as if expecting him to answer this time. But he didn't. I wanted to reach out and touch him, to feel his leg, to imagine a heartbeat somewhere within his chest. But I couldn't. Instead, we moved on to some other topic: Maggie Hensen's bow legs or the new family that moved in down the street from me. We'd laugh at how the mother was a dwarf-midget and her husband was a normal person.

We laughed often during those early days along the river, just the three of us. Every time I laughed, I would open my eyes for a moment and look over at him to see if he was laughing too. Only once did I think I saw a slight smile spread across his face, though I was never sure. Still today, I want to believe he did. It gives me something to remember with a smile of my own.

A month later, Janie's dad came home. He'd been in the army for as long as I'd known Janie; every time I went over for supper at her house, her dad would sit at the table dressed in his green fatigues, his hair shaved a short prickle-length that looked to shine white when the light hit it just right. His back would be straight against the chair, his elbows in as he cut at whatever meat had been served.

But there was something different with Janie's dad when he came back. He'd been gone for only a few months, but it seemed as if he had aged years. His skin now carried scars I hadn't noticed before; I was always too afraid to ask if he'd always had them. Though Mom never told me why, she said I was not to go over to Janie's house anymore for supper or sleep-overs. She told me that Janie was welcome anytime at our table and in our home, but that Mr. Phillips needed time to "adjust back to the world here," she said.

I remember how Mom and Daddy always watched the TV until late at night, sometimes even falling asleep on the couch while the news program played along with the commercials for Tang and Brillo pads and audio recorders and all other sorts of products that seem so ancient today. Each night, the news program would end with the newsman reading the names of the soldiers dead in Vietnam. I would listen to the names mentioned, creating a life-story for each: a wife and kids, a girlfriend waiting at home, a dog, even. In one of those stories, one of the dead men was the boy from the river's uncle; I imagined how, in his pack, the uncle carried fruits from the jungles there that he was going to give to his nephew when he got back. I imagined how, if there was an afterlife, the two of them might be sitting beside each other, munching away at the sweet fruits.

About two weeks after her dad came back, I started noticing the changes in Janie. She began coming to my window earlier in the mornings, tapping on the glass for us to go to the river. Those mornings, I would wake and put on a long dress that was mud-stained at the bottom. I would quietly climb through the open window and out into the cold wet morning. Without word, Janie would turn to the woods and take off, leaving me to run as fast as I could to the river. As fast as I could to our summer home.

On those river runs, I would hear the train's whistle from miles away. Its whistle sounded like an echo in the morning air, bouncing from tree to tree, and I believed if I closed my eyes and followed the sound of the train I would be led directly to the river bank and to him.

Janie began wearing makeup during those days. Blush and eyeliner, mascara that stretched her lashes to a dark and fake-looking length. It all seemed so different from the girl I'd grown up knowing. Her clothing also changed. She'd done away with the tomboy pants and shirts and now she wore skirts and thin tops, the outline of a bra on her shoulders and back.

It was during those days that Janie began construction on a house along the river's bank. The two of us would wander throughout the surrounding parts of the woods, collecting fallen branches and twigs; we would bring them back to the river and set them down gently on the ground for fear of waking him from his nap—we rolled him on his side during those scavenger hunts, with his right arm bent under his head to act like a pillow. He would be facing the river, listening to the current as he dreamed dreams that both of us, Janie and myself, secretly hoped we were part of.

After we collected the materials for three or four days, we began arranging the larger pieces of wood, stacking one on top of the other, building one wall, then another adjacent to it, until we had four walls that leaned up against each other and stood four and a half feet high. I had taken some rope and twine from Daddy's shed, and we used it to latch the branches and twigs together.

For the roof, we found long pieces of fallen tree. Most of these required both of us to carry together. Other pieces, we'd drag behind us, creating hieroglyphs on the pine-coated ground.

As we were placing one of the last branches on the roof, Janie said quietly, "I'm gonna live here with him. I'm not goin back."

I turned and watched her fit the branch beside the others we had put on earlier that day and the day before. She looked over slowly, as if noticing me for the first time.

"What happened?" I asked. I was afraid to know, afraid to hear the answer.

She breathed deep and then forced a smile, but there was so much sadness to it. "He wakes screaming in the night. Louder than I thought you could scream. I went to their door and looked in, and he was sitting up, screaming at something that wasn't there, and Momma was there too, holding him, hugging him tight. Last night I saw him throw her off the bed. Right into the wall. He was screaming and crying and I was and Momma was, too. I don't want him home anymore. I don't want him there."

Tears rolled down her cheek, and I walked around from the other side of our house to hold onto her and tell her it was okay, like I'd seen in movies. But she walked away before I got close enough. I watched as she went over to where he sat—we'd moved him so he was watching us work on our house—and she turned him so that the two of them were now facing the river. She put her arm around him and moved his arm so that it circled her waist. Her head rested on his shoulder.

I wanted to scream. To tear them apart. But I didn't. I couldn't. Instead, I sat down and watched the two of them, wishing upon everything that it was me beside him.

I've often thought about the destruction of the world and the things within it. I've often thought of our house, the one Janie and I never lived in—things seemed to get in the way. If I were to go to the river now, would it still be standing, some remnant of a home that never existed? Would I find him there still? We never said goodbye to him. Not properly, at least.

When school started in September, we moved on and left him behind, waiting for us.

***

It happened in October. Janie came home early from school; her mom was still at work. Janie walked into the kitchen and found her father slumped over the table, a spray of blood and brain painted on the wall behind him. Try as they might, the police and her mother never found a note, though I remember finding the truth out one spring night four and a half years later. Janie and I were on the outskirts of the valley that night. She went out there a lot of the time to "escape it all," she said. What that meant was she would drive the winding roads until she found a place to pull over and drink herself to sleep with stolen whiskey from her mom and step-dad.

She was already drunk by the time I drove up and sat in the passenger seat of her car. She smiled and reached over to the glovebox and pulled out a white handkerchief. She unrolled it sloppily and handed me what was inside: a small, folded piece of paper. On it, written in a soft, faded pencil were the words *I'm sorry for this. I'll always love you both.* She had taken it from the table right beside where his head lay, split in half by the .45 bullet. Janie told me there wasn't a single day in the four and half years since it happened that she hadn't opened the letter to read it. I believed her. Then I folded the paper up and handed it back.

The next few years passed slowly enough for us, and we both found ourselves moving along different paths, meeting and spending time with other friends. When Janie moved away from the valley, it was as if an acquaintance I'd known was leaving. She'd gotten pregnant not long after that night on the outskirts of the valley when she handed me the note—the beginnings of the bump showed beneath her graduation gown. On that night, with diploma in hand, I hugged her one last time. Balloons lifted high into the humid night sky while we all moved like ants bumping blindly against one another on the football field and the band continued playing "Pomp and Circumstance" long after the tassels had been moved over.

When she finally did leave the valley with Kyle and their daughter, Janie never called or stopped by. There was no chance for me to say goodbye to her, to wish her luck, or tell her what she really meant to me, even in those days when we were just friends from long ago, silently passing each other in the market and streets with gentle nods of recognition.

I think what I was most sad about when she left was that we never got a last chance to walk into the woods and make our way to the river where so much had happened and so much had been left unsaid and undone.

I moved from the valley, myself, five years ago. Not a day passes when I don't wish I had gone back alone to see him sitting there, looking out at the swirling water while life passed on behind his back.

So many times throughout my life I've thought back to him. I've wondered what he'd look like now if he were alive. I've wondered if I'd still feel the same longing for him as I did those days down by the river. I've wondered how it would be if I could look his name up in the phone book, drive over to his home and knock on his door, or watch him through the window. What would I say to him? What would I do? I wonder if he could have loved me. I wonder if I could tell him how he's been the one constant in my dreams since I was that little girl hiding behind the cover of trees all those years ago.

Stormdance

I stayed up all night with her when she was sick, tendin to her coughin, feedin her warmed broth from a can. I fetched blankets to try an help her sweat the sick out. Didn't do no good though. She died that next night, an I knew it was my fault.

Been two years since, but I find myself thinkin of it everday, specially days like this, when the skies out past the window gray up an they sparkle of rain. I feel her all round me, out in the wind an in the trees. Wish I could go out an call her back, tell her to come inside before the rain starts. Wrap her in a hug.

You can smell a good storm comin, Daddy says. You can hear it too, I reckon. I rest my ear up to the glass now, feel it vibratin under me. Comin quick, an I know it's gonna be a bad one, jus like that one two years back.

Daddy wasn't home then, Mama neither. Both was at work—Daddy in the shafts out under Sud's Hill, jus outside Corvin Valley there, an Mama workin at the postal office. Daddy was first to come home. Cain't member what time it was though, tell truth. He come home an find my sister settin there naked cept for the blanket roun her little white arms, she shiverin an shakin like a rabid pup, an me tryin to light the logs with a match. Those matches kep blowin themselves out in my twitchin, wet fingers. Rain water kep runnin down my nose from my hair. I could taste it, an I spat it out before me, riddin myself of that moment.

Daddy come an rushed past me, knocked me clean over, he yellin somethin, but I couldn't hear nothin nor see him none with the rain an tears in my eyes. Everthin was jus a blur, liken my dreams of that day, colors an streaks with no shape. Only thing I member was her blue lips an the way she stared straight forward like some vice was wrapped roun her head, cranked tight. But Daddy, he picked her tiny body up an took her on back into his and Mama's room. I stayed in the front room there, all lone with the thunder soundin heavy outside an all roun me. The rain runnin down the windows.

Mama jus come home now. I can hear her shoes squeakin loud over the floor. Feet wet already. "Storm's comin quick," she calls out, not sure to who. Daddy's still at work.

They ain't treated me the same since she died. Don't blame em; I ain't able to look in a mirror glass an be right with what I see lookin back neither. I hope some day I will, but I don't suppose it. Some things you jus cain't get shaked of, an you carry it roun with you jus like a scar you cain't see.

"Rain's comin down hard," Mama says. She walks into the room where I'm at. Stops when she sees me there, my head up gainst the glass still.

"Yeah," I say. I don't look back at her.

I woke that mornin to my sister tuggin at my arm an the sound of wind an rain outside. Was a Saturday an I wanted to sleep, but she pulled at me to take her out to the storm, somethin we done times before. "I wanna dance," she said. "Mama an Daddy ain't home."

I got up cussin her, an dressed. I made sure she was wearin her jacket an pants. Then we set out into it, me wantin nothin but to get back to bed.

First second or two's the worst of it, when your body jus starts gettin soaked through. Once that's done, you cain't feel the rain no more an it don't bother you none.

She lit off head of me into the woods. I tracked her for a spell an foun her standin next to the river's edge, she watchin the water explode on the surface of it. Had a smile on her face—I still see that smile when I close my eyes. She started dancin, kickin her feet this way an that, her knees jumpin up to her belly fast, feet comin down hard on the earth. Mud. Her arms was stretched out, beggin the rainfall an everthin that came with it. I watched her dancin an shoutin, actin like she controlled the air an water an the rain. Trees swayin to her feet.

After some time, she stopped an looked over at me through the storm. "Dance," she tol me. "Dance for the rain." I told her naw, that she was stupid for draggin me out of sleep like this an that I was jus as stupid for followin her. Tol her you wouldn't catch me dancin like no idiot in the rain, not like her. I was goin back home, back to the warm, I said, an I turned to leave. After some steps, I looked over my shoulder an saw her glarin at me, dancin even harder than before, jumpin higher now, comin down hard with anger. She wasn't dancin for the rain now, she was dancin in spite at me. Hate an love sketched all the same cross her face. Her eyes was closed an her body moved over the bank, an before I could call out to stop her, I watched her little feet dance right into the river an I watched her taken under the water, gone away.

Mama stands behind me now, lookin out the window at the storm. Our two faces close together. Lightnin glows the sky white. Thunder shakes the walls an glass. I can hear Mama whisperin a prayer next to me; she finishes an I look over to her. "Don't you be comin back here," I hear her whisperin, talkin quiet, like she's talkin to herself, like she's talkin back to the storm. "Don't you be comin roun here again." She looks at me now. I know there's love in her eyes, but it's mixed with hurt. An I cain't do nothin for it. I look back out at the storm. Rain so hard you cain't hardly see the yard in front of the house. The trees outside now all but disappeared, standin black out there gainst the gray an blue shadows.

I breathe in heavy an let it out. It fogs the window. An through the fog, outside in the yard, I see her, my sister. She's come down from the trees, out of the sky again. She's dancin there. I know it ain't real, but that don't matter. Not now it don't.

I walk to the front door an open it an walk out to the rain. First second or two's the worst of it, when your body jus starts gettin soaked through.

Mama watches me go.

She's quiet at first but then I hear her voice callin me back. But I keep goin. Thunderin's all about me, an Mama's voice jus becomes part of it all—jus sounds. An I don't hear em. Instead, like a whisper in all that bangin an shoutin an cryin, all I hear is my sister's voice. "Dance," she says. "For the rain."

I look up to the blackenin sky an I start. Mama's still callin me back to her. I see her face jus before I close my eyes.

My feet kick up high an my body turns in circles an my arms stretch above me, an I dance. I hope she sees me from wherever she is. Dancin. Dancin. My eyes're shut tight. I cain't tell if it's rain or tears runnin down my face. I know that Mama keeps yellin to me from the house, but I jus dance an call out to the world in grunts an sounds of song, an I dance an I dance an I sing to the sky.

One Last Time

When Charlie Gregg opened the door to see his younger brother Sammy on the other side, he knew something was wrong.

Charlie had just sat down on the couch and turned on the TV, finally settling on one of the numerous syndicated sitcoms that played every evening. His body was still wet from the shower he'd taken after work. The day had seemed longer than normal, tougher, laying concrete for the parking lot of the new market over between the two towns, Corvin Valley and Barrett. Charlie closed his eyes briefly and listened to the laugh-track playing on the sitcom, wondering if, in some way, the laugh track was meant for him and his own life.

His arms had the heavy, achy feeling he'd become used to over the past year of working construction. But today was different—his legs hurt and his head throbbed. There was also a pain in his stomach that he tried to wash away with a couple quick gulps of beer.

So, when he heard the knock on the door and saw Sammy there—the latter's eyes shifting around him uncomfortably, glancing first to his own feet and then to the left and right, seemingly searching the length of the trailer outside for someone hiding in wait—Charlie could only take a deep breath to quiet the pain in his head before letting Sammy in.

When they were kids, they found the body of a dead dog. By the time they came across it, the skin had begun to flake off from the bone. Fur, in clumps, had been pulled from the carcass and scattered around. Charlie reckoned it had been there for quite a while because it had no odor at all, none of the stink of the dead. When they came upon it, carrying the long sticks they'd just been using as light sabers, having just seen *Star Wars* in the theater with their grandfather, Charlie stopped and doubled over heavily, putting his hands on his knees. The thing before him in the dirt road was nothing but a darkened and coarse silhouette of something that had once been. Charlie had never seen anything so grotesque, so indescribably lost.

While Charlie, nine at the time, stood at a distance from the carrion, trying to understand what it was that lay before him, Sammy, two years younger, walked up to the rotted skeleton of the thing and began to poke at it with his stick. Charlie protested, telling Sammy they needed to leave and go home, that he should stop touching it, but Sammy only shook his head and reached down and picked up what was left of the body. Chunks of dried skin and small pieces of flesh, discolored from heat and time, fell from the lifted body. Sammy brought it up to his face to study it like a scientist would some newly found species. Maggots crawled within it, twisting their way slowly around the dry, brittle, gray bones; tendons were blackened and baked, pulled tight or snapped completely in two, flopping about.

Charlie took several steps forward but then stopped and turned away from Sammy. He bent over again and began to retch, feeling the bile rise in his throat, but the feeling went away quickly when he heard the sound. He turned back to his brother and saw that Sammy had thrown or lain the body, Charlie was not sure which, back on the ground and was taking the stick and slamming it with all his might down on the bones. Sammy was panting, a curious smile on his face that Charlie would never forget. After several seconds of smashing the thing, Sammy cast the wood stick aside and began to jump on top of the bones. They snapped below his tennis shoes, making sick crunching sounds. Sammy was sweating at that point, his face red, and Charlie could only look on in confusion and surprise. He wanted to do something, say something, but didn't know where to start. Sammy began to slam his heel down onto the skull of the dog and did so several times before there was a loud cracking sound and Charlie saw the skull separate into two separate but nearly equal parts.

Charlie often thought back to that morning and wondered if that was when it all started for Sammy, or if it was something that had always been there: the aggression, hiding in the recesses of Sammy's being, waiting to burst forth. Many nights, Charlie fell asleep with the image of Sammy jumping up and down on the animal's bones, the smile on his brother's face all the while. On those nights, before he rolled over and drifted off to sleep, Charlie wondered whether—if he were able to go back in time—he would have stopped Sammy that day. And, if so, would that have been enough? Would it have changed his brother from who he ultimately became and what he eventually would do?

Sammy sat on the wooden chair that Charlie brought over from the kitchen. Charlie sat on the couch, cattycorner to Sammy, and looked inquisitively at his brother. He offered Sammy a beer but, to his surprise, his brother only shook his head no. He looked Sammy over and noticed his brother was covered in a sour sweat that stained his shirt dark and made his skin look slick. There was also what looked like dried mud splattered over his pants and shirt, but Charlie paid it no mind after his brother sat down. Instead, Charlie broke the silence that settled itself between them. "What happened?" he asked quietly.

Behind them, outside through the open window, Charlie could see the sun finishing its fall below the pines. The sky held only the ghost of the sun's light, showing in streaks of orange and pink against a paling yellow-blue. Soon, those colors would disappear and only the blue-black of night would be left.

Charlie had moved out there several years before, after Maggie left him. He sold the small house the two of them had shared and bought the small trailer, pushing himself farther and farther away from people and from the towns. He enjoyed the company of the trees and the streams, the birds that called overhead, and the occasional deer that passed by; he sought and embraced the solitude these things allowed.

Sammy shook his head and then, finally, sat upright and looked at Charlie. "I need your help."

Charlie nodded. "Okay," he whispered. He moved his hands together, his rough palms making a scratching, sandpapery sound.

"It's bad. But I got no one else to ask."

"What happened?" Charlie asked again, this time more forcefully. He leaned forward on the couch.

"I don't know." Sammy took a deep breath and then let it out slowly. The sound echoed between them.

Charlie brought his hand up and rubbed his face. He thought briefly of his head and how it no longer hurt, though the sick pain in his stomach was still there.

Sammy stood quickly and began to walk around the small room. He moved his fingers gently over some of the pictures that lined the walls. All were of their family, their mother and father and the two of them, Charlie and Sammy. He sighed. "It's Mullans. I screwed things up." His voice raced now, as if it were trying to catch up with the constant stream of thoughts that worked their way through his mind. "I owed him and I screwed things up bad. I don't know what I'm supposed to do."

"How much did you owe?" Charlie shook his head as he asked.

"Eighty."

"Jesus. How?"

"Shit, I don't know. It just piled up til I was that far back. He cut me off after the last job and I had to borrow some."

"And, what, you didn't stop borrowing?"

"It just happened. And then today I went there . . . Charlie, I—Goddamn. I don't know what to do. He . . . Ah, shit. I screwed it all up. I screwed it up. Shit. Shit." He took another deep breath and shook his head. He looked over at Charlie and smiled, though the smile was full of pain, confusion. It was a smile Charlie had never seen from his brother, a smile that showed that Sammy was in true trouble and, worse yet, that Sammy knew it. Then his brother said, in a voice so controlled and calm that it scared Charlie, "I messed up, big brother."

* * *

Sammy had met Mullans after he was released the second time. The first time, he only stayed a couple days in the local jail from a bar fight, though the man he fought had lost an eye and a few teeth.

He served sixteen months for the second arrest, this time for armed robbery of the bank; he used a neon green squirt gun, saying later that he'd never meant to take the thing out of his pocket. The water pistol was found out only when it fell from his jacket and clanked to the floor after an off-duty tackled Sammy from behind.

After he was released, the court set Sammy up with a job in the mines. Though he hated the job, he showed up every morning on time and worked hard until the whistle blew the end of the shift. He'd been working there for five months when one of the other men in the mine, someone he'd not seen before, came up to Sammy and asked to talk with him at Roy's after work. When Sammy asked what for, the man only smiled and said he knew someone who could help him out.

When Sammy showed up at the bar, he ordered a beer and looked around the dimly lit room for the man from earlier, but he saw no sign of him. Sammy finished the beer, waited another ten minutes, and then headed out to his car. When he made it to the parking lot, Sammy saw the man from earlier standing under one of the dull lamps that lit the lot. Beside him stood another man.

"I waited for you," Sammy said. He tried not to sound as frustrated as he felt.

"Seemed a better place out here," the man from earlier said.

This man introduced himself as Tom and then introduced Sammy to the other man, who he said was named Mullans. This man was in his late fifties, tall, a good head above Sammy, and skinny as a rail. Sammy wondered briefly if there was something wrong with the man's health, but reckoned that maybe he just didn't like eating much, and Sammy didn't think anything else of it.

"Let's take a drive," Mullans said. His voice was higher than Sammy imagined it would be. Sammy nodded reluctantly and unlocked the doors of his car, a beat-up orange Ford, twelve years old. The three men got in and Sammy started the engine and then pulled out of the parking lot.

Mullans didn't say a word the entire drive. Instead, Tom directed Sammy where to go. The entire way, Sammy cursed himself, wishing he was never in this situation, wishing he had just gone home after work. He wondered if they were going to kill him, although he couldn't imagine why. But he realized he had no other choice and so he kept driving. When he asked where they were going, Tom only answered that they were going somewhere safe and that everything was fine.

They finally came to their destination: a cabin in the woods. Sammy drove slowly over the winding path that led to the place and came to a stop just in front of the small porch. Tom and Mullans got out of the car, and Sammy followed slowly behind. Mullans turned back to Sammy, welcoming his guest to his quiet home. Sammy nodded and followed the two men up the short steps and into the cabin.

The three sat at a table in the kitchen. There, Mullans finally spoke again. He asked Sammy if he liked working in the mine and Sammy replied that he didn't but that he had to under court order. Mullans laughed, saying that he had quite a few connections throughout the area and that if Sammy didn't want to work in the mines, then he didn't have to anymore. Sammy sat quietly, thinking of what to say. After some time, he asked why Mullans was helping him. The man responded that he was not helping Sammy as much as he was helping himself. Mullans told Sammy that one of his employees had recently moved away to New York City and that he needed someone else like this previous employee, someone strong, tough, not afraid to test the law or get his hands dirty.

Sammy shook his head and smiled, saying he didn't think he was right for the job. He was about to stand and leave when Mullans told him the pay. When he heard the figure, Sammy sat down slowly and shook his head. He took a deep breath and then let it out slowly. He looked up at Mullans and smiled. "Where do you want me to sign?"

* * *

Charlie drove while Sammy sat in the passenger seat, watching the darkening night pass by. Sammy took a long drag off a cigarette, opened the window and flicked the thing out; then he rolled the window back up.

Charlie's heart beat fast. His arms and legs had lost their soreness and his stomach was now free of its previous pain. He shook his head, wondering what strange turn of events, what error in the ways of the universe or what unkind god put him in this place he now found himself.

Charlie remembered when Sammy first told him about Mullans. It was the night before Maggie left him, though Charlie had known for weeks that she was readying herself to go. Sammy had taken them both out to dinner, something that never happened, and he told them about the meeting and what was said there. When Charlie asked, Sammy said that it was technically legal, though beyond his own dealings in the job, he wasn't so sure. Since that night, every time Charlie brought it up, Sammy would smile and look away, saying that everything was good, that he had no complaints.

The road stretched before them, cutting through pockets of trees and forest. Sammy rolled down the window again and this time stuck his hand out, letting the warm night flow around his outstretched fingers. Outside, Charlie could hear the call of dogs or wolves; he could not tell which. These sounds seemed to steady his breath some, and he forced himself to focus on the drive.

"You walked this whole way earlier?" Charlie looked over at Sammy.

Sammy met Charlie's glance briefly and then nodded. He didn't say anything. He looked back out the open window and closed his eyes, letting the wind sweep over his face.

After another ten minutes, Charlie turned the car off the main road. Sammy opened his eyes and reached over to turn the knob next to the steering wheel; the headlights went dark, and everything around them was thrown into heavy shadows. Above them, the moon glowed brightly and came down in streaks that were cut through by the branches above them. Sammy thought of how the shadows formed prison bars that lined the stretch of dirt they now drove. Charlie slowed the car to an almost standstill, and they made their way along the path to the cabin that they each knew lay ahead.

The lights were still off in the cabin, and Sammy was glad for this. He went in first, his hand gripped tightly around the .45 he had taken from the bedside table earlier. Charlie kept close to his brother. Sammy said that there would be no one coming by until the next morning, but he told Charlie this only to calm himself and assuage his own doubts. The front room held only a couch and a giant television. Beyond that was a large wooden bar area equipped with barstools and a trophy case of alcohol. They turned to the hallway on the left, just before they reached the bar.

Sammy walked slowly, his feet soundless on the wood floor under him. They passed two bedrooms on the left of the hall and a small bathroom on the right. Sammy held the .45 out in front of him, listening for the sounds of someone else in the cabin. Silence. Nothing.

Charlie felt cold all over; his breath came in short, strained efforts. He thought of all the other things he would rather be doing. He thought of Maggie, remembering the feel of her body next to his. He wondered how she was now. He hadn't talked to her in months, and the last time they did talk he had hung up the phone angrily. He now cursed himself for doing so and promised that when this was all over he would call her up and say he was sorry for all that he did and all that he didn't do.

Finally, Sammy came to the last room on the right of the hallway. He stopped before it and eased the door open all the way, then looked around inside. From his pocket, he pulled a small flashlight and shined the beam around the room; he still held the .45 out before him, as if the thing could ward off the demons he expected to find there.

After Sammy made his way completely into the room, Charlie followed. It was the sour, coppery smell that first struck Charlie. The sick feeling in his stomach came back, stronger now, and made him double over and cough. Sammy looked back quickly, trying with his eyes to shut his brother up, but the room was dark and Charlie couldn't see Sammy at all. Instead, when Charlie stood up, he could only see the mess in front of him, as the beam from the flashlight was directed there. Lying half on and half off of a low wooden bed, was the body of a man. Charlie could not tell what the man looked like, as all that was left were stained rags of clothing covering the body, deep pockets of a caved-in skull, and pools of blood that looked black in the dark room. The wood flooring, for several feet surrounding the body, was splattered with blood, and a river of it ran from the crushed head and collected near the door. "My God," Charlie whispered.

Sammy looked over at him.

"Mullans?" Charlie asked, motioning quietly to the body before him.

Sammy nodded.

Charlie looked back at Mullans, but, try as he might, he couldn't truly decipher what he was looking at. He couldn't even begin to comprehend how a person could become this mess of skin and bone and gore; nor could Charlie begin to think how a person was capable of doing such a thing to another person. And, for the first time in his life, he truly looked at Sammy with fear. Sammy didn't notice any of this, as he had already set about undoing the sheets from the bed. Sammy stuck the flashlight in his mouth, which caused the beam of light to jump all about the room in a frantic movement that seemed to only add to the disorder and confusion of the moment. After he took the sheets and blankets off the bed, Sammy began wrapping the body up in them. He looked up from what he was doing. The beam from the flashlight fell on Charlie, blinding him and forcing him to turn his head away from the light. Through clenched teeth, Sammy whispered forcefully to his brother: "Grab a towel and hurry. Clean it up. We gotta hurry."

Charlie nodded and turned quickly, moving fast and loud to the bathroom down the hall, where he grabbed three dark brown towels from under the sink. He returned to the bedroom and began to mop up the red-black liquid. Sammy finished wrapping the body and moved off to the closet on the other side of the room. Charlie could hear his brother opening and shutting drawers. The light flashed quickly over the room and Sammy returned, carrying in his hands a new set of sheets. He began to make the bed with these sheets, tucking the corners under the stained mattress. All done with such care.

The towels had become heavy, and Charlie put the used ones on top of the body, which lay next to where he was crouched. After he finished, Charlie stood and helped his brother make the bed. They laid two large blankets over the sheets, covering up what had happened there, the truths and secrets now buried beneath fabric.

Without a word, Sammy and Charlie grabbed the wrapped body and lifted. The bundle was heavier than either had guessed, and they struggled as they moved through and around the door frame and down the hall to the outside. They set the body in the trunk of Charlie's car and closed it; then they went back inside the cabin. Charlie took another towel from the bathroom and mopped up the remaining blood that had collected under where the wrapped body had been. Sammy looked at the bedside table, over to where a clock flashed the time; he thought about putting the .45 back where he had taken it from, but then he thought better of it. He shined the light over the entire room once more, and thought that, from a distance at least, no one would ever know what had happened there.

They walked outside, making sure to shut the door behind them, and then got into the car. Charlie drove off under the moon's light toward the main road.

Charlie stopped the car about halfway back to his trailer, pulling onto the shoulder of the road and turning off the engine and lights. They made sure no one else was driving by before they opened the trunk and, once again, unsteadily lifted the wrapped body from inside. They walked into the deep thicket of trees that stretched miles beyond where they were and dropped the bulk on the ground. Charlie ran back to the car for the shovels they had taken from his home earlier. He gave a shovel to Sammy, and the two set to digging, turning over the softened dirt and piling it in a mound. Neither spoke; the only sound was their breathing and the steady hum of the cicadas and other chirping bugs in the trees around them. This sound seemed an ocean that would swell loudly before tapering off and become gentle, only to return to its heavy buzzing once again.

As they were nearing the end of their job, the hole now a good four or five feet deep and about the same in length, Sammy spoke. "I went over to talk to him, ask about getting more work, you know? But he didn't answer when I knocked. It was early still, and, shit, I didn't even know he was there. And then, next thing I know, I'm inside the house and then there I am, standing next to him, next to the bed where he's all passed out. And then I saw the needles there on the bed, his arm still all wrapped, and knew he was already passed out. And then . . . Shit. Then, I swear to God, next thing I see is him slumped over on the floor and my hands all covered in blood and my boots covered in blood from where I had kicked down, and I was sweating and panting like I'd just run a mile. And I walked down there to the creek there behind the place and washed my hands and my feet and clothes and shoes, and then I headed for you, because I couldn't think of no one else . . ."

Charlie couldn't hear Sammy after a while. Instead, all sound seemed to drown out, and he looked up and noticed that here, in this place, the canopy of branches above was too full for any moonlight to escape through. And he thought of the dog from all those years before—the smashed frame that remained after they left. Charlie thought of how they were only a few hundred yards from where they'd found the dog, and he wished he could go back in time, dig a hole for the dog and cover it with earth, and say a few words over its grave. But he couldn't; he could only dig this hole now and hope that it was enough.

When Charlie pulled up to his trailer, it was nearly 3:30 in the morning. He cut the engine of the car and the two sat in silence, neither wanting to be the first to open the door, neither knowing what to say to the other. After several minutes of this, Sammy rubbed his right hand over his left. Charlie wondered if Sammy's hand hurt from beating Mullans earlier, or if this was just a nervous movement his brother made. And Charlie thought then of how he had never really known his brother, and how he never would.

After sitting in silence for several minutes, Charlie opened the door and let it close behind him. Sammy followed and then moved over to where Charlie stood outside the car. In the moon's light, they each saw one another as they truly were in that moment: scared, dirty, alone, confused. Charlie nodded and began to move toward the front of the trailer but stopped when Sammy called his name. He turned and was caught off guard by Sammy's arms wrapped around him in a true embrace; it was something that Charlie had never experienced from his brother. But Charlie was most surprised at how comforting it felt to be within his brother's arms; part of him wished he could just disappear into Sammy's haggard shirt, one covered in blood and gore and dirt and time and regret and every other emotion he could think of.

When Sammy finally let go, Charlie was left standing alone again, his body feeling heavier than before, missing the extra weight of his brother, like a phantom limb. Sammy nodded and turned to walk off into the dark of the night but stopped and looked back at his brother, one last time. When he did so, Charlie tossed his keys out into the dark toward Sammy and heard them hit the ground just before his brother's feet. Though he couldn't see Sammy's face, Charlie imagined it held a look of surprise and happiness, and this image made Charlie smile.

"Sam." Charlie's voice was steady and quiet. "Go north." He paused. "Or south. Or anywhere else. Just go and don't come back, okay? And don't tell me where you've gone or when you get there or how you are."

Sammy slowly nodded in the darkness and bent down to pick the keys up off the ground. By the time he stood again Charlie was already inside the trailer.

Charlie heard the car's engine turn and then the tires as they rolled over the ground, kicking up dirt and rock pebbles and crunching sticks into pieces. He didn't turn to lock the door, he didn't look through the window or anything else that might cause him to see his brother driving into the dark world that awaited him.

* * *

In the shower, Charlie scrubbed his body with soap. Dark water fell from his skin, and pieces of debris, remnants and reminders of the night, collected in the drain, and he knew he would need to pick these things up later and throw them in the same plastic bag he had shoved his clothes into moments before.

Closing his eyes, he looked up at the shower spout and felt the water hit his face. He looked down after a few minutes and wiped his eyes. He hadn't realized it earlier but he was crying, his tears merely blending in with the shower water.

Charlie finished and stood naked in front of the mirror. He looked at his reflection, judging it, weighing its worth, though what he weighed it against, he was unsure. He slowly put on a clean shirt and shorts, smiling at the fresh smell. He made his way back into the front room and sat down heavily on the couch. His arms and legs hurt, and the headache from earlier was back.

In the darkness of the room, Charlie looked over to the small table next to the couch, over to where the telephone sat in its cradle, remembering his promise from earlier to call Maggie. In his mind, he heard the steady buzzing of the phone's ring, the click of it being answered, the sleepy "hello" and the awkward seconds where he tried to think of what to say. But then he thought of what he would say when she asked what he had been doing. He couldn't answer that. He thought he might say, "Helping Sam with something," though that would not be enough and he knew it.

This battle raged in his mind for several minutes. He closed his eyes and focused on breathing, feeling his heartbeat slowing. He reached over and picked up the remote control from next to him on the couch and turned on the TV. The room, which had been dark and silent just a moment before, was now changed, thrown into a fabricated reality of color, the joyful sounds of the program surrounding him in the small room.

As he sat there in that skewed reality, Charlie thought of Sammy driving through the night, the windows rolled down and the air whipping his hair about his face. He thought of Sammy's left hand stretched out into the night, his hand closing into a fist and then opening, as if he were releasing air that he had caught back out into the world. He smiled at this thought, and he found himself forgetting everything else that happened before. And he let his eyes close to the image of Sammy driving away.

Avenues

Dad told us a story once, and it's stuck with me ever since. I was maybe ten—Andy would have been twelve, I guess—and Dad sat us on the curb outside the house and pointed off to the right, over to where our street ran into a tangle of other streets and avenues that had names I couldn't pronounce.

"It was just down there. I was just a few years older than you are now," Dad said. He had a far-off look in his eyes, like he could actually see himself in that moment, young and thin and innocent, with the world in front of him still. "Wasn't a day went by I wasn't picked on, beat up by the kids round here. I'd come home with blood running down my cheeks and lips, staining every shirt I owned. I'd walk in the house and drop my bags and go straight to the bathroom to stop the bleeding so my mom, your grandma, wouldn't see."

Me and Andy sat there, neither of us moving. Here Dad was, letting us into this world we never knew existed; it was a world neither of us wanted to know about. "Their big thing back then was to steal shoes off kids' feet. They'd tie the laces together and then sling em up so they'd hang on the telephone lines. I lost a good twenty shoes that way." He smiled, though I can remember now how it was a strange smile—not the kind that comes from real happiness but something else. I think now that it was pain.

"So, one day," he said, "I'd had enough of being beat down by them. It was after school and I made sure they were all out in the street when I walked by carrying two shoes at my side. I yelled out to em all, 'Hey,' I said"—he actually yelled that out to the empty street while we sat there on the curb—'Hey, look what I got,' and I held up those shoes. When they asked where I got them from I told em it was from a punk kid at school I didn't like. I took the laces right then and there and tied em together—my hands shaking like a mess the whole time—and then I threw them up to that line." He motioned up at the telephone line that stretched above our heads. "Those shoes caught on the first try, but I didn't look up. Instead, I kept my eyes straight ahead at the kids that would beat me up every day. I saw them all staring up at the line and those dangling shoes, and I smiled. They left me alone after that, thinking I finally became one of them." Dad drew his lips tight then. "I don't think any one of em noticed me walking back to my house barefoot." Dad finished his story and looked away. Still to this day, I remember tears in his eyes, but Andy always held to the fact that Dad never cried at anything, that day or any other.

I don't really know why I remember that story now. I guess I've been thinking about it a lot these last few years. Or maybe it's what Dad said to me later that night when I asked him about the story. It was just me and him in the kitchen; Mom and Andy were already upstairs. Dad put his hand on mine—something he hardly ever did—and said, "Sometimes it's better to act like you're something, even when you aren't. It's how you get by sometimes."

I think Dad might have been talking about Andy then, though he didn't know it at the time. Luckily, Dad didn't live long enough to realize this. Though not a day goes by for me that I don't think on it.

Over the years, Andy and I drifted apart. It was my fault more than his, I'll admit it. Once I got to high school and the comparisons became more regular, it finally hit a point when I couldn't stand it. Always in his shadow, whether it was school or sports; every day it would be some comment about why I couldn't do something the way he did. In their eyes, I could never live up to him. But they didn't know what I knew about him.

A week after graduation, I went my own way. I boarded a bus with a small duffel bag over my shoulders, not caring where it was headed, just as long as it was moving away from Andy and everyone else I'd ever known.

I rode the bus east for ten or so hours, watching as the cement and buildings of the city faded away into suburbs, with their neatly built houses and grass lawns all the same pattern. Then the bus passed into a wooded land covered in a blanket of green—trees so thick you couldn't see your way through them. Eventually those trees disappeared and all that was left was the ocean and the dark beach that stretched alongside the water. It was only then, when I saw the expanse of it all, when I looked out across the water and couldn't tell if there was anything out there for me to truly see, only then did I realized how, for the first time in my life, I was alone. And I remember how I smiled at that thought.

Mom would call me once or twice a week to check in.

Dad died when I was a sophomore in high school, and, ever since, Mom's devoted her life to the church. On those calls, she'd tell me about the women at bible study; they were all older than she was, each with kids and grandkids, and Mom'd tell me all about them, as if I was supposed to know these women on a first-name basis. I always thought that each mention of babies and grandkids was a hint to me, but I knew just as well as she did then that Andy was the one who'd have kids and a family. Not me. I guess it was just a hope for her, though.

Every few months, I'd get a letter in the mail from Andy. I'd read over the words, judging him more and more with every sentence. My mind would bring me back to that night and I'd feel myself growing angry, sweat beading on my forehead, tears starting in my eyes.

"I've grown up," he wrote in the last letter he sent. I knew he had because he signed his name "Andrew." I threw the letter away before I finished reading what else he'd written. I can't tell you how often over the past few years I've thought back on that letter and wished I'd read the rest. I wonder if there might have been some clue to it all that he'd left for me in his words. Something that might at least give some answer.

I was in the middle of my graveyard shift at the docks when Mom called to tell me Andy was dead and I needed to come home. I remember feeling the weight of the phone in my hands; it seemed to grow heavier with each passing second I stood there.

After she told me, I nodded and looked off to the ocean. The water lapped against the concrete and wood of the pier, sounding like a drum keeping time to that moment and to my emotions. "Okay," I said. That was all I could say. And then I hung up and went back to finish my shift.

The next day, I took the bus back home. Out the window, I watched the slow progression of society and time: the ocean giving way to the green of the woods and then to the suburbs and finally the city again with the haze stretching out above the gray buildings like a dirty halo. The entire drive back I ran over different scenarios in my mind: car crash, heart attack, stroke (like Dad), accident at work (but then I realized I had no idea what Andy did for a living). Why hadn't I asked Mom how he died? Was it to protect her from telling? Or was it to protect me from hearing? To distract myself, I looked out the window and watched the flashes of color: men and women walking the gray sidewalks, their coats of blue and black; schoolgirls in white sweaters and tan skirts and pants; a soccer team on a green and brown field, their uniforms red with mud-splattered patterns that whirred by too quickly to study. The darkening of the afternoon. The end of something. What was to come next?

It was night when the bus pulled into the station. Our house was a half hour's walk away, and I set out with my duffel bag slung over my shoulder. I moved slowly around the corners of my childhood, down the avenues and boulevards of my youth.

Graffitied brick walls ran parallel to the dark streets. "My streets," I'd once called them. "*Our* streets," Andy had echoed. But that night, coming back to them, they were unfamiliar. It had been too long to know them anymore. As I passed by The Charles

Street Diner, I reached out and let my fingertips bump along the brick wall there—rough on my skin—wondering how much of my sweat and saliva was still speckled there, hidden beneath the dirt and grime and spray-paint.

After a while, I came to the house. It looked the same, though more worn and, like everything else I'd noticed since coming back, it was dirtier than it used to be. Weeds and grass of yellow and brown poked through the cracks in the sidewalk and street. I'd always remembered the house larger than it was, and when I knocked on the front door, I could hear the hollowness inside.

After she opened the door, Mom hugged me a long time but didn't say anything, and then she turned and walked into the house. I followed her, closing the door gently behind me.

It wasn't until after I set my bag in my old room and gone to the bathroom that she spoke. She was sitting at the table, her hands in front of her, one over the other, with only the kitchen light on. The counter and the table-chairs threw long shadows on the dark floor. Years ago, I would have run away from those shadows, thinking they were ghosts stretching out to grab hold of me. Now, though, I realized that the only ghosts and demons in the world were those things you can't see. The things that make no real sense. The things that can't be explained.

"I'm glad you're here," she said. Her voice sounded deep and scratched. I could hear the sadness in it. "Me, too," I said, and then she put her head down on her hands and began to cry. I watched her shoulders rocking up and down with sobs, but I couldn't move. There was nothing I could do or say, and so I simply watched her cry for the brother I had run away from.

When I was eleven, I watched Andy walk out from the gym where he'd played basketball for the high school—varsity his freshman year. My parents would tell everyone they could about him being on the team. There was always pride in their faces when they talked about Andy; their bodies stood more erect and their smiles seemed more genuine. I always felt like a shadow on the floor behind them in those moments. A ghost. Eventually, I would walk away and busy myself looking at birds flying above in the afternoon sun or I'd try to count the stars in the night sky. But that night, as my parents were congratulating some other kid's parents on the game, I watched Andy walk toward us. I don't think he saw us waiting because, for the first time in my life, I noticed he wasn't smiling. He always walked around with a smile so big it looked glued to his cheeks with construction paper. Instead, that night, his face was blank, angry even, like there was something missing from his eyes that was normally there. Only when he looked up and saw the three of us standing in the parking lot, Mom waving to him and Dad clapping for a good game, did Andy smile and let out a laugh, erasing the stranger I'd just seen.

I've found myself doing that a lot these last few years. I look back and replay the moments in my life when I was with Andy. Like a detective, I look for anything that could give reason to why he did any of it, but I normally catch myself before I get a headache from thinking too hard. I tell myself it's pointless. That there's no real answer, no matter how hard I try, and, even if there is, what would I do with that answer? Would I call Mom up and say, "Hey, I know why Andy killed himself. I know why he killed her, too." Would that do anything? Would that bring back the smile that's no longer on Mom's face? Would that get rid of the gray hair and the lines around her eyes and her cheeks? Would that keep her from crying herself to sleep every night?

The night I came home, Mom and I sat in the front room. I ate a plate of microwaved lasagna she made the day before. She told me what she knew, what anyone knew at that point. She'd talked to Andy on the phone two mornings before; he sounded tired but good, she said. He was working at some law office in the city doing clerical work. He was dating a girl named Marianne, a Spanish girl Mom liked. Even then, with all that had happened, with Andy dead, she talked about him with so much pride. I couldn't understand it, and I wondered if she ever talked about me like that.

Mom said she had come home from bible study when she got the phone call from the police. She told them they had the wrong number, but then they described Andy's body, the scar on his wrist from where he'd fallen from his bike when he was six, the strawberry birthmark on the back of his left shoulder. They said they couldn't tell her what his face looked like because most of it was no longer there.

Marianne was on the couch, a pillow over her face, her hands over the pillow as if she were shielding herself from the world. She had been shot twice. Andy was only a few steps away from her, his body sprawled on the ground, the gun still in his hand, his index finger still hooked around the trigger.

After the memorial service, I went to the apartment. I looked at the walls, the faint red and brown dotted spray covering them, knowing it was the last remnants of my brother left in this world.

Nights as a kid, the sounds outside our window would scare me. Tires scraping hard over the pavement, feral cats rummaging through metal trash cans. Horns blaring from the avenues a distance away, the drivers headed to places that only existed in the stories I heard told.

I'd cry softly into my pillow, feel my body shivering in a cold fear and then, a minute or two later, I'd feel Andy climb in bed next to me. He'd hold my hand and I'd feel his skin touching mine. Warmth. Comfort there. "It's okay," he'd whisper to me. I'd close my eyes and drift off to sleep and lose myself in dreams I never could remember, knowing the entire time that Andy was there to protect me.

I loved Andy in those moments more than I loved anyone else.

Mornings after those nights, I'd wake and find Andy already eating breakfast at the table downstairs. He'd look up from his spoonful of cereal and smile at me. He'd take another bite or two and then ask if I was ready.

We'd slowly walk to school, our eyes trained upward, tracing the telephone lines in search of Dad's rotted shoes.

Every night the year after Dad died, Andy and I would sit on the curb outside the house. The sun would set, throwing the sky into a multitude of colors constantly bleeding one into another. Oranges and yellows gave way to reds and then violets and blues, and finally black. Neither of us would say a word. Instead, we'd listen to the music of the world around us, believing Dad was the conductor of it all. Each car backfire a bass drum, each car engine strings to the orchestra. The night birds roosting in fireless chimneys called out to the moon were the wind instruments. The whole of the world around us was alive, and it only made sense to believe that Dad was alive in it all, too.

It's been nearly six years since Andy died. Two years ago, I met Evelyn. During the first few dates, I'd look across the table at her, the dim light of restaurants throwing shadows across her face. I knew the shadows were doing the same to my own. Portions of us hidden from each other in those moments, and I would wonder how much of our lives are really hidden from others.

I like to think that I can be honest with Evelyn. I thought I could then, too. But it wasn't until we'd been together for three months that I told her about Andy.

We were sitting on one of the wooden benches that line the beach walkway. "Why don't you ever talk about your family?" she asked.

I looked away and shrugged my shoulders. "Not much to say."

She was quiet for a few seconds, so I looked over at her. "I'm here," she said.

That day on the bench, I told her about Andy and how he died. I told her that no one knew why, that the not knowing was the hardest part of it all. She only nodded and then reached out and put her hand on mine—something she does so often now.

Recently, I've found myself thinking more and more about Andy. I don't know if it's this secret belief that by me remembering him, remembering the parts of our life that no one else knows, that maybe he can't disappear completely. That maybe I can remake him into someone I always wanted—someone I thought he was when I was a kid. I hope that just maybe I can help him.

Not long ago, Evelyn asked me why I hated Andy so much.

I told her I didn't. Not anymore.

"But you did."

I nodded.

"Why?"

"Because I couldn't save him." I turned away from her. Then I repeated those words. Not to her, but to me.

I can still remember it if I close my eyes tight enough.

The room was dark, no moon in the sky. I woke in the middle of the night and listened to the sounds outside my window, the sounds that had brought me such fear when I was younger. I lay there listening to the back alleys' voices speaking to each other. Then I heard footsteps somewhere else in the house. I got out of bed and walked into the hall that connected my parents' room to Andy's room on the other side of the house. I could see Andy's door outlined in a faint glow of light.

Walking toward his room, I could hear the sound of muffled crying. As I crept closer to the door, the crying grew quieter and I wondered if Andy had heard me. I kept still, holding my breath, afraid I might be found out. Then, after a while, I continued on until I was just outside his door.

Through the open crack, I watched as Andy sat on the floor in front of his bed. He was dressed only in his boxer underwear and he was holding a pillow to his face. I could tell from the movement of his body that he was crying still. I wanted so desperately to go in and throw my arms around him, hold his hand and whisper that it was okay, just like he'd done for me so many times when we were younger. But I couldn't move. Dad's propane lantern was a few feet away from where he was. In the dim light, I watched as Andy put the pillow down on the floor beside him and wiped the tears from his eyes. Then he turned and reached under his bed. I couldn't tell what he brought out but I could see he was holding something small in his hand. It was a blade, I could tell. Then he slowly raised the blade to his leg and dug it into the skin. I could see the blood run in tiny rivulets down his thigh. I could see the tears in his eyes. Then he raised the blade to his other leg. I wanted to run in, scream at him, tear the thing from his grip, tell him it would be okay, hug him or hit him, but I didn't. I only watched him through my own tear-fogged eyes.

If I had run in, would it have changed anything? I ask myself that a lot of the time.

Back in my room that night, my chest burned from holding my breath so long. I wiped my eyes dry but it was useless with the new tears that streamed down my cheeks. And so I sat alone on my bed and cried, not for the pain I saw in Andy's face, not for the blood or the fear I felt watching him. I cried, instead, for some other reason I've only just now begun to understand.

Last night, I rolled over in bed and looked at Evelyn as she slept. Her hair was swirled all messy over her face. I wanted to nudge her awake. I wanted to have her sit up, look at me and ask what was wrong. I wanted to cry and let her hold me in her arms. I wanted to ask her if it was my fault, if all of it was because of me. I wanted her to tell me that it wasn't, that some people do things for no reason, that no one could have known he'd do something like that. And I wanted to tell her that I knew. That I'd known for as long as I could remember. But I realized as I looked at her that I would never be able to bring myself to tell her what I'd seen that night all those years ago. I couldn't tell her how I'd seen the pain in Andy's life. I couldn't tell her I'd seen how lost he was and that I turned away. I'd heard people tell me I wasn't as good as Andy, *Why can't you be him?* they'd ask me when I knew what he really was: a liar keeping secrets and pain from the world.

Now, looking at my reflection in the mirror, I realize just how similar me and Andy always were. I think back on what Dad told me that night. *Sometimes it's better to act like you're something, even when you aren't. It's how you get by sometimes.* I've only just started to wonder if maybe it wasn't Andy he was talking about. I'm starting to wonder if maybe it was me.

In the Woods

When my daughter asks about her mother, I tell her about the children of the woods. "Who was she?" my daughter asks. "Where is she now?"

"She's one of them," I say, though my daughter is too young to understand what that means, and that's a good thing. The risk of scaring her with what will someday be causes me too much pain.

At times, I catch myself looking out the window at the moon—the bright sliver of it hanging so perfectly in the darkness there. I often wonder if we're cursed, our village, though this is how life has always been, and how it will continue to be.

Like all fathers here, when my wife was pregnant with Laney, I was full of emotions: excitement and fear. And sorrow. Sorrow so impossible to express.

One night, I lay in bed beside my wife, my finger tracing circles on her swollen belly. Then I stopped. "What's wrong," she asked. "I'm scared," I said. She knew what I meant. "I don't want to lose you." She brought her hand to my face and kept it there for a long time, and though she spoke no words aloud I could hear them in my mind. *Shhh. It will be all right.* And then we fell asleep that way. I often think back to that moment, realizing how it was the closest she would ever come to being a mother.

* * *

It is a practice in our village.

After the birth of a child, the doctors take the newborn to clean it. The mother is sewn up, if needed, and then two or three nurses take her to the woods. The nurses who escort the mother stay a distance from the tree's edge, not daring to cross over into the darkness of the shadows, into where the wild callings of the children sound.

After the nurses walk away, the new mothers walk or crawl into the woods and join with those who've gone before. In the woods, the mothers' bodies are transformed, changed over time into children who shriek and holler in the long summer nights. With each passing day, the baby grows older and stronger and the mother becomes younger, one day to one year. And this backward-aging continues for the mother until she becomes a feral child, and she remains in that form forever. We were told by our fathers that the mother gives her life over to the child in this process, that she allows all the good to be passed on.

We are a village of men and children. Those women still here await the births of their own children so that they too can pass on their being to the next generation and rejoin their kind in the woods.

Sometime in the future, my daughter will marry and have a child of her own and become like her mother, leaving me alone. I try to accept this fate, though I cannot. I know it's the movement of our life here, but the fear of losing the only two things I've ever cared for is too strong.

Most nights, I stand outside my daughter's room. On the other side of the door she sleeps and dreams about the horses of the fields or the fish within the sea. Maybe she dreams of her mother, like I do. I'll stand there awhile and then, after several minutes, I'll make my way back to bed and fall asleep.

On nights when I can't sleep, I find myself walking alone through the streets of the village until I come to the edge of the woods. I've never told anyone, but I continue into the darkness of the trees there. Until I find the children.

They gather in one of the many clearings. I'm guided there

by the dull glow of the bonfire that grows bright as I continue to walk. And in the glow from the makeshift fire, they stand or sit or dance around to some unheard melody, some beat that keeps their feet pummeling the dirt and leaf beneath. After a while they stop their dance and look up to the sky. And there, they paint themselves in brilliant golds and blues against the darkness of the universe. From a distance, they look like crustaceans moving over sand, their hands raised in triumph at their immortality or loss for what they can never have back.

There's no telling which it is at any moment.

A Lovely

The air was cold. Snow gathered in bunches on the tops of the bare trees and icicles stretched downward from the branched fingers.

A fog came from the little girl's mouth as she stood there, silently staring at the small boy; frozen, he was tangled in the web-like branches of the bushes down near the creek that was iced over with small, skinny fish swimming just below the glassy surface. The boy's eyes were closed and his mouth parted slightly as if he were peacefully dreaming a sleep he would never awaken from.

"Found him down near the water out in the woods some distance in. Frozen clean through," the doctor said. He looked at the body of the boy lying on the cold metal table. The boy's skin was a faint blue color, his arms resting at his sides. The doctor looked back up at Jackson Shaw, Corvin Valley's mayor.

"Who was it?" Shaw asked.

"Don't know. Don't believe I've seen the boy in my life. Haven't heard of any missing children neither, from our town or any other. You?"

"No, no. I haven't, but I mean who was it found the boy?"

"Oh. Mary-Beth Watkins's girl. She was out playing hide and seek or something like that. That's what Mary-Beth told me, at least."

"In this weather?" the mayor asked, looking around at the small, cold room.

"No school. Gotta keep busy somehow," the doctor responded. He shrugged his shoulders.

"How's she holding up? The girl."

The doctor scratched the side of his stubbled cheek. "Good as can be. She doesn't think much about it, as much as I can gather. But then again, I only talked to Mary-Beth for a bit this morning. It's still new to the girl anyhow, fresh. And she's too young to really understand much, but we'll keep an eye on her, either way."

Shaw walked around the table, examining the boy from every angle, until he was standing beside the doctor. "And you haven't heard of anyone missing?"

"Not that I reckon, yet. I'll keep asking around, though. If you want."

"No need. If someone's looking for him, they'll find him here. When we hear from them, we'll let them know then. Things like that always seem to work out."

"Okay."

"And I don't want to stir anything up much. Seems a waste of energy sometimes."

The doctor nodded.

"But still," Shaw reached slowly down and laid his swollen fingers down on top of the boy's small, frail ones, "Still is hard on anyone." The skin was cold and reminded him of plastic. "But I'll be damned if he doesn't look familiar."

Shaw shut the door behind him and untied his scarf. "Maggie! I'm home," he called out. The house was silent. He hung his coat and scarf on the hook by the door, stomped off the loose snow, and walked into the dining room.

His wife sat on one of the wooden chairs, looking out the window at the white winter beyond the glass. Snow was beginning to fall again, light and drowsy now. He walked to where she sat and rested his hand on her shoulder. She jumped a bit, startled by his touch, and then turned to face him. "I didn't hear you come in."

He smiled down at her. She looked blankly back and then turned her head to the window. They stayed like that for several minutes, each watching the sun set over the white peaks of the valley walls, each of them separate from the other.

"I thought maybe it would be good to get you out of the house." Shaw had already finished his dinner and now took an extra roll from the plate and was wiping it through the leftover gravy.

"I don't want to. Not now, Jackson. Please."

"Maggie. It's okay. I know it's hard for you now. I do."

"Do you, Jackson? Really? It seems as if you're fine with life. With everything!" Her voice rose to a shout and then settled back down to a whisper. "I can't just forget it." Her hands were shaking and she laid them palm down on the table to stop the movement. "I can't. I can't."

"I'm not fine with it, Maggie." He looked down at his empty plate. "I never will be. But I've realized—especially who I am in this town—that I need to move through it. Every year. It's one thing to mourn, but it's another thing to destroy your life over it. What life are you living for him if you keep like this? I mean honestly."

She was silent. She looked away and then back at him. Her cheeks were wet with tears. "I know, Jackson. I do. But I can't. It's just too hard to let him go."

Jackson settled back in his chair and watched her.

She stood and collected the plates from the table and took them over to the sink and began to wash them. Except for the ticking of the clock in the other room, the house was quiet. After a while, Maggie looked at Shaw. "Okay," she said.

He stood and walked over to her. She was holding her hands under the sink, the hot water running over them, turning them pink and soft. Steam rose in the air before her. Shaw turned off the faucet and put his hands on her shoulders and she began to sob. He turned her around so she was facing him and guided her head to his chest. And they embraced, each holding the other as they had not done in years.

They lay next to each other in bed, silent. Neither knew what to say. They had sat and watched the news on the TV and then turned off the lights. Both could hear the other's breathing, Jackson's was more strained than hers. "Do you need your inhaler?" she asked.

"No. I'm okay."

She nodded and then rolled over so she was looking at him. She studied his face, its dark silhouette lined against the room's white walls, the moon's glow filtering through the blinds. "Would you like to have lunch tomorrow?" Maggie's voice broke. "If you can't, if you have something already, then I understand, that's fine, you know. I just thought . . ."

He cut her off. "I would love to."

"Yeah?"

"Yeah. Why don't you come over to the office at twelve forty-ish." He smiled.

"Okay," she said. She smiled, too. Then she placed her hand on his chest and he reached up and held it there while they both fell asleep.

Shaw was sitting in his office when the phone rang. He picked it up. Tina, the receptionist from down the hall, was on the line. She told him that the doctor was on the other line and needed to talk. "He says it's important," she said, "but he didn't say what it was about." The mayor told her to put the call through.

The doctor sounded as if he were out of breath. He told Shaw that he needed to see him.

"What about?" the mayor questioned.

"Just come here. As soon as you can. It shouldn't take long, but I just need to show you something."

The mayor hung up the phone and grabbed his coat and walked out of the building, telling Tina he was going to the doctor's office and that he'd be back to the office within the hour.

The doctor's office was only a few blocks from the small City Hall building. Shaw decided to walk instead of drive. The sky was clear and the new snow on the ground sparkled and seemed to light his way. He looked at his watch and saw that it was twelve twenty. He hoped the doctor wouldn't take long; he didn't want Maggie to have to wait.

* * *

Shaw walked into the small office. The doctor was sitting behind his desk; several books were scattered in front of him—some opened, some closed—and he was thumbing through a tarnished medical journal. The doctor looked up.

Shaw took off his coat and laid it on the back of one of the chairs opposite the doctor. "The girl up front told me to come in."

The doctor nodded and smiled.

"So, what's going on?"

"Just come with me," the doctor said, as he stood and set the journal down on the desk, adding it to the rest of the clutter. He walked out the door quickly, not waiting for the mayor.

As the two walked down the dimly lit hall, Shaw noticed the smell in the air. "Did you just paint?"

"No. Just the heaters acting up. It smells like that in the mornings when they kick in. We can't run them all night with the prices, so we just start them again every morning."

Shaw nodded.

The two reached the end of the hall and went into the elevator and rode it down to the basement level.

"How's Maggie?"

"Okay." Shaw looked down at his hands. They were cracking and raw from the cold weather.

"I know it's the time again." The doctor looked at his watch, then looked over at Shaw. "How are you?"

"I'm alright. I still think about it, but then I try to move on with it. You know? I don't know if that makes me wrong or bad. I don't know. But I try not to let it wear me down. But Maggie's different. She's . . . Every year, this week, she just shuts down." He shook his head and then took a deep breath. "Every year it's the same thing. She doesn't eat anything, hardly sleeps. Last night was the first. Usually she just sits in her chair and stares out the window, like he's out there and she's waiting to see him and hear him come home, and she waits and waits, but he just doesn't come. Honestly, it's been eating away at us. Constantly. Both of us. It's changed who we are to each other."

The doctor nodded. "I'm sorry, Jackson. If you want, I can make a call. I know a good therapist. Really. She's helped a lot of people."

"No. Thanks, but no. We've tried talking to someone about it. And it goes away for most of the year. Occasionally it creeps up on her—you can tell it docs—but it's okay enough for the most part."

"It's hard, I can only imagine. And I can understand why this is so hard on you, being five years. It's a long time. Some people just can't let things like that go."

"Yeah." Shaw took a deep breath.

They reached the bottom and the elevator doors opened. They walked out and down another hallway, much like the one from the floor above.

"And I think things would be different if we ever, you know . . ." Shaw's voice trailed off, seemingly afraid of what the rest of the thought might hold.

"Found him," the doctor finished for him.

"Yeah."

"I understand. It's the not knowing of it. Most people, like you, can accept it and move on, but for some people it's harder to do that. Acceptance comes only when the mind's willing. I wish I could tell you something that would help. But, if you need anything, just know that I'm here. We all are." The doctor gave a sympathetic smile and then looked away.

"I know. And thank you. I mean it." Shaw patted the doctor's arm gently and smiled a sad smile.

They stopped at a door halfway down the hallway. The doctor fumbled with his keys. He finally unlocked the door, and they both entered the small room. Jackson followed behind as the doctor walked toward a large set of metal doors. The doctor opened the doors and walked inside. A few seconds later he came out, pushing a gurney with a white sheet covering a body. The doctor pushed the table over to Shaw and uncovered the body. It was the boy from the previous day.

"Have you heard anything yet about any missing boys?" the doctor asked as he balled the sheet up and set it on the ground.

"Nothing yet. Someone might call soon, though."

"Maybe. Hopefully. Anyway, I was doing some checking around this morning, trying to get a better feel about him."

"And? Find anything?"

"Well, judging by the look of his skin, the complexion, I'd say he was out there some time. It's hard to say exactly, but it had to be a while."

"Okay."

The doctor continued talking. "But then, when I looked closer, I found that the internal organs had all been frozen solid, the blood in the veins, too. I've never seen or heard of anything like this before, with freezing to this extent."

"So, what does that mean?"

"I don't know. It would have to mean that the exposure time to the temperature, the freezing conditions, was for an extended amount of time—years even. But there's no way he could freeze like that. It doesn't get that cold. And still, I doubt he would be in such perfect condition. A body exposed to the natural world for that amount of time should be completely destroyed—weather, animals—but, here he is, in an almost perfect condition. Preserved. It makes no sense. It's impossible."

Maggie opened the door to the doctor's office and walked over to the short, blonde-haired receptionist behind the desk. She smiled at her. "Hello."

"Hello, Mrs. Shaw. What can I do for you?" the receptionist said, moving some cluttered papers on the desk and looking up at the woman standing before her.

"They told me at my husband's office that he's here with the doctor."

The receptionist smiled. "He came in a little bit ago. He's still with the doctor. You can wait here, in the lobby…"

"Is he all right? Where is he?"

"I believe the doctor and the mayor are speaking on private matters."

Maggie smiled slightly. "No, I'm sorry. They're old friends. Nothing is ever private with them and nothing is ever important, but I need to speak with my husband. That's important. Where can I find him?"

The receptionist smiled. "Of course. Let me check for you." She lifted the receiver off the desk and pushed some buttons on the number pad. She stayed silent, listening to the phone for several seconds before replacing the receiver. "They aren't in the doctor's office, but they may be downstairs. I'm sure he won't mind if you go down." Then, she added quietly, sarcastically, "If you *need* to speak with your husband now, then by all means, please feel free."

"I do. Thank you." Maggie turned and walked down the hall to the elevator.

Maggie gently opened the door. The two men who had been huddled together over the boy's body looked over, startled. They each took a quiet breath when they saw Maggie.

"I'm so sorry about this, Maggie. I needed to come over on some business, but I think we're done for now." Shaw smiled and walked over to her. He hugged her closely to his body, but she remained stiff within his arms. Behind him, the doctor was covering the body of the boy with the sheet.

Maggie looked past her husband to the table. "Who's that?" she asked, to no one in particular. "What happened?" The doctor looked up with a helpless expression at Shaw.

After a second, Shaw looked at her and smiled sadly. "It's just someone who was found in the woods. We don't know who it is yet. We don't want to spread a panic by announcing it just yet, until someone reports something."

Maggie looked at him; her face was set tight. "How can you not tell people? How will you know who he is, who he belongs to, if you keep it secret? Jackson . . ."

The doctor began to roll the table to the back room again, but Maggie hurried over and stopped him, holding the table tightly. "How has no one claimed him? How horrible . . ." But she stopped short when she moved the sheet from the boy's face. A low sound rose from her throat and tears welled in her eyes. "My God. Jackson." She looked up at her husband and then back down to the boy; she stood over him, quietly holding her trembling hand to her face.

"Do you believe in second chances, Jackson? This is our second chance. He is our chance. I know it. I feel it. Can't you feel it? It's in the air. It smells—flower petals, spring water. I don't know. I mean, I know it sounds crazy." She smiled. "My skin feels it, though. Here. Touch my skin." She directed his hand to her arm. She laughed. And then tears began to fall down her cheeks. A moment later she stood and then ran out of the restaurant, leaving Shaw alone at the table, unable to do anything but watch her leave.

When Shaw returned to his office after lunch, he sat in the chair and looked at the pile of papers on his desk. He moved them aside and put his face in his hands. His breath came sharp and quick and his chest hurt. His body felt as if it were shaking, his fingers tingled, and his head seemed to expand and then shrink and expand again.

After a few minutes, he picked up the phone and dialed the doctor's office. "I don't know what to do now. She's lost everything, everything. It's not there anymore."

"What happened?" the doctor asked, quietly.

"At lunch, after we left the office, she began to go on and on and on. She thinks its Adrian. She thinks the boy's him. And she's just . . . I don't know, I really don't know. Just tell me what to do. She thinks she's found him now."

The doctor was quiet for a minute, and then he told the mayor that he would be over in a few minutes. Shaw set the phone down and looked at his hands in front of him. They were clammy with sweat.

Minutes after the doctor walked in and sat down in Shaw's office, the phone rang. Shaw answered it and handed the phone to the doctor. It was the receptionist from his office telling him that something happened, that she saw a woman carrying a white sheet out through the parking lot toward the woods. Just before she hung up, the girl on the phone said, "I think it's the mayor's wife." The doctor looked at Shaw, confusion crossing his face.

"What is it?" Shaw asked.

"I . . . I don't really know. But I have to go. Someone took that boy."

"Maggie?"

Without answering, the doctor stood and walked out of the office; Shaw followed close behind.

The two got in the doctor's car and drove to his office.

He parked the car near the edge of the woods that surrounded the outskirts of the town and got out. They walked briskly through the trees, the snow soaking through their shoes, their socks becoming wet and cold. They stumbled occasionally through the large piles of snow, following a path of footprints left there by some other traveler before them. They walked for a while, neither saying anything. After several minutes, they came to the small creek that was glazed over with ice. The surface shimmered in the sun and a few shadows covered the glass surface in dark strips from the trees. There, sitting along the edge of the water was a woman. Propped up next to her was the boy. They were both sitting on the white sheet. Her arm was around the boy and they seemed to be looking off in the distance, to some other time or place. The two men were quiet in their approach and they stopped a few steps behind the woman; they were each breathing hard, fog rising from their mouths and disappearing into the air.

Maggie was gently running her hand over the boy's cold arms. She was telling him about the vacations she had taken, about parties and weddings, about family and friends, children she had seen in town and how they could be friends of his. She talked excitedly about the boy's upcoming birthday and how sad she had been for his other birthdays, but how special this next one would be now that he was back home. She moved her fingers through the boy's hair, moving some strands from out of his face. And she talked of the pets they now had, the dog and the cat, and how well the two of them acted together, and how the fish they'd had had jumped from the bowl and she began to laugh as she told him how the fish couldn't stand swimming any longer and wanted to try out his land legs.

And then she positioned the boy's head so that it leaned up against her chest and she took a deep breath. "Shhhh," she said quietly, soothingly. "Close your eyes. It's all okay now. It's all okay. Everything is all right again. You're home now. I love you. Shhhh. Shhhh."

De-Programming

She knocks, and I yell for her to come in. As she closes the door behind her, the phone rings again and I quickly lift the receiver from its cradle and then set it back down, disconnecting the caller. It's the fourth time I've had to do that this hour.

She walks over and sits down across the desk from me, smiling the same Should-I-go-through-with-this-? smile they all have when they come in for a consultation. Like almost all of our customers, she's fat, though she's a different kind of fat from the others. She could be pretty, like really beautiful, if she weren't carrying the extra hundred pounds or so around. Still. I look at her bulging cleavage and think about Meredith. I wonder where she is right now. I wonder if I would still love her if she were fat. I tell myself I would, but I'm not really sure if that's true.

I know the woman's been talking to me for the past five minutes, but I'm too lost in my memories to hear a single word of it. After a few more seconds of thinking back on the past, I look up at the woman and smile, realizing she's waiting for me to answer her.

"What's that, again?" I say. I rub my eyes with the palms of my hands, hoping it will fool her. *Oh, he's had a long day,* she'll think. If only she knew.

"I was just asking when you could come out for the . . . appointment?" She stutters over the last word, not sure what to call the whole thing. I don't really either.

I open my planner and flip to this week. I see that Saturday is Meredith's birthday. I had planned a weekend away upstate: wine tasting, watching shooting stars over the mountain tops—an escape from all of this here. I sigh softly at the thought. "Tomorrow I'm free," I say as I look up at her. "That work for you?"

She nods. I smile. The kind of smile that got me this job.

"Alright, then," I say, and we stand up together. I lead her over to the door. "I'll see you around nine tomorrow. Okay?" I hand her one of the brochures that sit on the table by the door and tell her to look over the details. "Make sure he's comfortable."

She thanks me with a hug, pulling me tight against her. We stay like this for a few seconds. I think she's about to tear up and use my shirt for a Kleenex, but she finally she lets me go. "I know he would be so ha—" But the ringing of the phone cuts her short. I see her look at it, a terrified quiet now taking over the room. She doesn't move, afraid of who's on the other end of the call, maybe.

Me, I chuckle silently and give her two gentle taps on the flabby arm. "It's okay. It'll take some getting used to for you, but you'll get it. Just remember, they're on your time."

The whole while the phone's been ringing.

"Aren't you going to answer it?" she asks. There's actual confusion in her eyes; I can see her lower lip quivering a little. I almost feel bad for her.

"No. It rings throughout the day. Part of the job," I say, offhand-like. "Sometimes I answer, othertimes I don't."

She looks at me with eyes now slits from her scrunched and fatty face. She doesn't understand. "But what if it's your mother?" she says.

I tell her it can't be my mother. "My mom's still alive," I say.

My apartment seems so much larger now without any of Meredith's things. She left just over two months ago and I still can't find my way to the bedroom. Instead, I usually sleep in my clothes from the day—I wash the uniform every other night, standing naked in front of the washing machine while it clangs away. Today is laundry day, so I throw the clothes in and hit the start button. The washer rocks on its base. I know I need to adjust the load, balance its weight, but the sound is a welcome change to the quiet.

It used to be that Meredith would do the laundry for me. I'd wake in the morning to a freshly folded uniform—work pants and shirt. I would dress while listening to Meredith in the kitchen making breakfast, and we would sit there across the table from each other, neither of us needing to say anything. Sitting there and chewing at our eggs and toast seemed enough. Though now, looking back, I guess it wasn't.

After I move the wet clothes to the dryer, I walk over to the kitchen. There's still nothing in the fridge so I grab the box of stale cereal from the counter and take it over to the sofa. I turn on the TV and eat my dinner, chomping down on the dry flakes. I wash it down with tap water from the sink and then take another handful and bite down.

Eventually, my eyes close and I can feel the cereal box falling from my hands. I let it fall, knowing that I'll wake in the morning to flakes of rice cereal crunching under my feet and getting lodged between my toes. A few seconds later, though, the phone rings and my eyes shoot open. I look over at the wall clock and see that it's just after 1:00 am. The room is dark; the only light I can see is through the closed blinds. I know it's Mr. Schmidt's apartment across the courtyard. Every night, he turns his room into a disco and waits for his wife to call. I watch him sometimes from my window. He sits on the couch and lets the bright lights of the disco ball twinkle and twirl around him while he laughs and laughs into the phone—I can only imagine at what. I've tried substituting words aloud in a fake conversation, but my German accent's off and I usually just stop and silently watch him talk to her.

I installed his phone two years ago. I take some pride in that.

Right now, though, it's my phone that's ringing. I never quite know what to do—answer or not—but after having neglected the sixteen calls at work today I feel like I've ignored it long enough.

I lift the receiver to my ear. "Hello?" I say quietly, waiting to hear which one it will be.

"I fucking hate you, you prick bastard."

"Hey, Georgie," I say calmly.

"Fuck you, man," Georgie says. I shrug, knowing he can't see me. "You know I woulda made it through."

Jesus, I think to myself. *It's been four and a half years.* You think he'd let it go, just a little?

"I know, George"—he hates when I call him that—"but you gotta realize, it wasn't my call. It was hers. You know that, man."

"I know. I know," he says. "I still hate you, you motherfucker."

"I know. I'll talk to you later," I say and hang up.

There are six of them that call most of the time. My "regulars," I call them. At work, me and the guys swap stories about our regulars. It's all part of the job, I guess. A lot of us de-programmers don't have phones installed at home because of them, but I thought, "What the hell?" At first, I hated the calls—they come at all hours of the day and night. Each time the phone would ring, Meredith would turn to me. "Really? Can't you just leave the job at work," she'd say and then turn away. I would apologize to her and then go answer the phone, if for any other reason to quiet the apartment.

Georgie's finally settled down from how he used to be. Don't get me wrong, he's still plenty pissed, and I can't say I blame him, but he used to say some pretty messed up things that even I was a little freaked out about. I almost de-installed my phone from one of those early conversations with him. I'm glad I didn't, though. Since Meredith left, the calls have given me some company.

Besides Georgie, there's also Alex. He's the most recent one. I like him—he's shy and quiet. I think he might be gay. I'm waiting for him to hit on me, but he hasn't yet. Alex calls about once a week, and we usually talk about different places we've visited or always wanted to visit. A lot of the time he hangs up crying, wishing he had had more time in life to visit Europe.

One of my favorites is Ms. Francis. She took forever to go down, yelling and swatting at me the whole time. I was worried how she would end up on the other side, but she seems good. I think she understands it was for her own benefit (she was dying of some cancer, I can't remember which kind). Every time she calls me, it's like she really wants to know how I'm doing. I tell her my troubles and she usually chuckles that deep, beautiful laugh only black women have. She's helped me with Meredith leaving. *Let the bird fly away, and if it flies back then you know it's yours.* Though it's cliché and probably a lie, it makes me feel good. "I wish I could have met you before, just to thank you," I tell her. She laughs and then tells me she'll bake me something soon. I don't have the heart to tell her that's not how it works.

The Tomlinson boys call every once in a while, usually asking sports scores. They were a sad one. I got there just in time for them. They were one of my few accidentals—that's what we call them when it isn't by appointment. Both of them were playing hide and seek in the front yard with their brother—they used to be triplets. The two of them were hiding behind the car when the third one jumped inside to look for them. The kid accidentally popped the brake free and the car rolled down the driveway, right over the two of them. They're sweet kids. If I ever have children, I hope they're like the Tomlinsons.

Finally, there's Samantha. She calls when she's all hot and bothered and "wants to feel up on me," she says. Samantha was a strange one—I got that call out of the blue a while ago. She said her sister was sick and I needed to get there quick to install. When I got to the house, though, Samantha was sitting alone on the couch, watching a lit candle in front of her slowly burn down. "Where's your sister," I asked. "Right here." She smiled. I told her it was against policy, but she said it didn't matter, she wouldn't tell. Then she slipped me an extra hundred and I agreed to it. She went peaceful under the pillow—hardly a fight at all.

Nowadays when Samantha calls, she usually just bitches about how there's nothing for her there. Says she misses it on the living side. "But I don't blame you," she tells me. "I wanted it then, I thought." I hope she's smiling when she says it, though it's hard to tell. Besides Georgie, Samantha calls the most, probably twice a day. I used to answer each time but now I don't. In truth, I think Meredith left because of Samantha. But I don't tell her that. She doesn't need more to hate about herself.

The entire drive, I look at the house-lined streets of suburbia. Nearly every house has one of our signs out front, advertising away for us like we are some security company from the old days.

It always surprises me how people take pride in having had us install a phone for them. There's so many protesters these days—usually a dozen or so out front of the office any given afternoon. "Murderers" their signs read. But they don't understand. It's a job for us, first-off, and, secondly, we're helping to ease those people's pain. Honestly, I was worried about it when I started the job, but after going through my first procedure and then getting the call from him afterwards, hearing his voice, strong again, like he was a fit forty-year-old, it was a no-brainer.

I smile at that memory. That was the same day I met Meredith. She was just sitting on the park bench eating a peanut butter and jelly sandwich when I walked over to her, feeling a mile high for getting my first real job.

I shake the memory from my mind and focus back on the directions to the appointment. In front of one corner house there are two signs—signaling two customers (what we call them)—and a banner stretching between them. On the banner reads our slogan: "Give us a call, so they can give You a call!" The house looks familiar and I try to think back to whether I was the one who installed the line there, but besides the Tomlinson boys, I've only done one other two-fer, so I know it wasn't me. Mark must have been the one. He's always so damn lucky when it comes to the calls he gets. He had one family of four, a mom and three kids—all of them burned in a house fire. The husband/dad called us up and asked if we could help. He was at work when the fire happened and said he couldn't stand watching them in pain anymore. I was about to head over when my manager told me Mark was right down the street from the house. Lucky bastard's all I can say about Mark. Plus, that husband/dad gave him a tip and a half for the installation. Even called into the office to tell my manager how "kind" Mark was. That's bullshit. Mark's the biggest dick I've ever known. But, hey, I guess he can play the game right, and I'll tip my cap to that.

When I pull up in front of the house, I see an American flag flying at three-quarters height. I breathe deep and grab the paperwork from the passenger seat and then go around to the trunk and get out my bag with the phone box and cables inside. I look at my watch. It should take about an hour and a half, all said and done, so I'll be able to make it to Regina's Diner before they stop serving breakfast.

When I knock on the door, Mrs. What's-Her-Damn-Name answers, still wearing a nightgown. *Jesus*, I think. *Couldn't even dress up to see him off?*

But it all makes sense when she leads me to him.

He's lying there on the bed with four tubes sticking out of his body—one shoved down his throat, two connected to his chest, and the last one a normal IV in his arm. His eyes flutter every now and then, but I can tell it's more than just sleep. The good thing is that he won't put up a struggle. That's one of the reasons we all tend to fight over who gets the comatosers. I'm guessing she probably told me the situation yesterday in the office during my mind-wander, so I play it off like I was expecting to see him like this.

The small room smells like socks and musty, old sweat. I set my bag down beside the bed and then look around me. Sunlight filters through half-closed shutters, drawing slatted shadows onto the carpet. On a chair in the corner is a crisply folded shirt and pants, camo fatigues. A camo hat sits on top, boots set neatly on the carpet. I'm sure if I were to look closely at the clothing, I'd see blood still from whatever made him like this. Near the headboard, beside the bed on a nightstand, is a framed 8x10 photo of Mrs. What's-Her-Damn-Name and the guy laying in front of me. She looks about sixty pounds thinner in the photo. Normally, I try not to look at things like photos—too personal for me to want to know—but I squint in the semi-darkness and see that the two of them have their cheeks pressed together, cheesy grins on their faces. In the foreground, almost blocking his face, are their hands held up to the camera, both of them showing off their new wedding rings. I breathe deep, feeling a wave of nausea come and then go. I turn and smile sadly at her, just like they taught me. "How long's he been like this?" I ask.

"He came back three months ago," she says. "Doctors say he won't get better from here."

I want to ask how it happened, but I don't. Instead, I just tell her to give me an hour or so and then I'll be out to have her sign the paperwork. She nods. Then I tell her if she wants to say anything, then now's the time, but she tells me she already did earlier. As she walks out the door she stops and turns. There's a smile on her face. I know what she's about to say. They all say it. "I'll talk to you soon," she says to him, and then she shuts the door.

I kneel down and take the equipment out of the bag and place it on the carpet. I begin to connect the wires to the phone. Then I take the small power drill and carefully make the holes in his temples and feed the other ends of the wires into his brain. When I started the job, I couldn't get the drilling down, but now I do it so there's hardly any damage done—the mortician will be able to hide the holes without problem. Next, I turn the battery pack on. It makes a slow, loud, clicking sound. It's at this point that most people come barging into the room, wondering if something's wrong. Then I have to shoo them out and tell them everything's fine—it's such a hassle. Andm as if on cue, I hear the door creak open behind me. I turn and see her standing there. Her eyes look puffy, but I can see that there's the trace of a smile still left on her face.

She asks quietly, "Can I watch?" Only one other person has asked me that question. That was two years ago and I told him no, but I look at her standing there in her oversized nightgown and, for some reason I don't understand, I tell her she can if she wants.

A few more minutes pass while the battery charges completely. When its charged, I turn back and tell her she might not want to look, and she nods her head in understanding, but she doesn't turn away. I reach down and grab the pillow and place it evenly over his face. Though there's not much research, we use a pillow to do it—whether the person's conscious or not. It's old-fashioned, sure, but there's always been worry that the way they go out is the way they'll stay on the other side—if we drug them, then maybe they'll make prank calls to their loved ones, all loopy and babbling away. If we do it another, more violent way, then maybe they'll be assholes when they call, and how awful would that be to get a call from your dead husband or wife or brother or whoever and have them perpetually be in a shit-mood? No one wants that. So, we use a pillow.

I press down hard and his body begins to spasm. It's all involuntary movement, I know that, and I hope that she does, too. The last thing I need is some crazy housewife screaming at me for killing her husband just as he was about to miraculously break free from his terminal coma, but luckily she stays quiet. After a few seconds, the spasms slow down and there's only small twitches. I turn back to her. Her face is set stern, though her eyes are squinched together; I can tell she's holding back the tears and I find that I am, too. It's strange. In that moment, for the first time, she seems beautiful and real. She reminds me of Meredith standing there, and I realize now just how much I miss her.

I smile a sad smile at this woman and then mouth the words, *It's almost over.*

And she nods.

The Orchard

Though a rooster just now crows from one of the many hidden coves of the valley hollow, the old man has already been awake and sitting on the porch for several hours.

In the darkness of the early morning, he wears a quilted blanket wrapped tightly around his shoulders and chest. The blanket still carries her scent, even after all the years, and he breathes it in deeply, hoping to be drunk on it. He dares not wash the blanket, soaked as it has become in dirt and grime, sweat and tears. He cannot lose all trace of her, for without something tangible, something once felt by her skin and tasted by her tongue, then all that is left are memories that will one day fade away.

From where he sits on the porch, Martin Weller regards the white of the moon in the distance, set off just to the east in the lightening sky, and then rubs the cold skin of his arms under the blanket. He feels the bumps and wiry hairs of age under his fingers. Already, there is the wet, sticky feeling of humidity on his skin—a constant in the valley during summer months.

In the distance of the land is the orchard, and he watches as its expanse of hidden parts becomes revealed in the morning sunlight. Martin smiles at this. *Another day. So much history out there, so many memories*, he thinks.

How must the world have looked in its beginnings? The time before, when there was void and darkness and nothing. He thinks this and then he looks at the boy sitting on the porch beside him.

"Like this," the boy says. And the old man nods.

"I reckon so," the old man says. "I hope so."

As a young boy, Martin Weller would follow his father as he walked the maze of the orchard. Martin would carry a metal pail and try his best to stretch his step out so that his foot fell within the impression of his father's boot on the dust-ground. The golden fruit would surround them on those walks, hanging just so on the outstretched branches. How easily Martin could reach out and take one of the apples and eat it, despite his father's warnings.

Martin was nearly nine when his father left for the war in Europe. His father knelt down in front the boy and told Martin to keep watch over the orchard. "It's yours to look after til I get back." And then his father kissed him on the forehead and climbed into the car that waited to take him away to the train station. The boy watched as the car drove the winding dirt road toward the city, and even after the speck of car had disappeared, after the dust from the drive had settled back to the earth, the boy continued to look off in the distance, simply imagining his father in that moment.

Three months later, his mother received the telegram. "Killed serving his country and defending the world from the Nazis," it read. His father's body was never recovered, never brought home. Lost at sea from where his ship was destroyed, they were told. Martin and his mother held a quiet ceremony in the orchard, just the two of them. They burned one of the trees that they'd ornamented with his father's favorite clothing and hats, the umbrella he often carried with him as he strolled through the orchard, the pocket-watch Martin had always thought would one day be his. In that moment, for the first time in his life, he said goodbye.

The years after his father's death, Martin spent most of his time in the orchard. He'd collect the apples that had fallen from the branches, dropping each bruised fruit into a pail to be taken down the road to Mr. Jessup for his horses. Often on these walks, Martin would pluck an apple from the tree and bite into it. The fruit would sound loud and crisp, like wood snapping in two. The juice from each bite would spray his cheeks and nose and dribble down his chin, and he'd lick the sweet from off his lips and smile, knowing that no one was around to see his joy, except maybe his father. And that was fine with him.

In many ways, Martin could always feel his father out there in the orchard, a constant guide to the boy and then to the man, as he grew.

He'd always hoped that his father would one day emerge from the mists of the field and join him on one of his walks within the orchard. Or that he'd one day walk out of the house in the dark of the morning with the blanket pulled tightly around him and find his father sitting beside the chair instead of the boy. Martin often imagined how the two of them would sit beside each other: an old man and his father, the latter a man half Martin's age when he died all those years ago.

But his father has not come. Not yet, at least. And Martin doubts if he ever will.

Martin's home and orchard are tucked away within the woods, some fifteen miles from the small town of Barrett. The surrounding rock cliffs look down upon the valley floor and cover his home in shadows.

Years ago, the town of Barrett would host a small fair at the high school on Friday nights. Families would gather and walk the brightly lit field, fathers laughing over a shared whiskey flask while children scattered about and won prizes at the gaming booths. In the early days, you would only see a handful of the valley citizens each week, though, as time passed, the fair drew a larger crowd until the mayor and town-council decided to make the fair an annual tradition, hosting it during one week in late September. Still to this day, the fair in Barrett draws crowds from all around Appalachia.

Though he did not normally go, a young Martin Weller found himself there one Friday evening, surrounded by both faces he recognized and others he had never seen before. He wandered the field with no direction, walking past gaming booths where children shrieked in joy and over to the booths that sold trinkets and artwork and other wares.

One of these booths sold pottery, and Martin stopped and held a bowl up to the light of the moon, tracing the ceramic's whorling patterns with his finger. He lifted the bowl to his nose and breathed deeply in, smelling a faint scent of pinewood and jasmine. When he set the bowl down, he saw a girl, several years younger than he, watching him. She smiled and laughed, and he turned to leave, embarrassed. He'd gone three steps before realizing he still held the bowl in his hands. When he turned to go back to the booth, he saw the girl standing before him. "It's the gloss shine," she said. He shook his head, not understanding. "That gives it the smell." He smiled and gave her the bowl. "I like the smell, too," she said, and handed the bowl back to him. "Don't worry. My gift." And then she turned and walked back to where he first saw her standing.

The next Friday, Martin, again, went to the fair. He walked slowly toward the pottery booth, scouting the distance before him in search of the girl. She was handing an old woman a tall vase, smiling kindly at the shopper. Martin stopped and moved over to the shadows of one of the gaming booths. He was not sure how long he stood there, watching her at her trade. People came and looked at the pots and bowls, vases and plates. When she laughed, she turned her head to the side slightly and smiled upward. She seemed happy, and he could not pull himself away from watching her. It was as if her joy became his own that night.

At ten o'clock, the booths closed for business and games. The townspeople made their way to the exits, but Martin continued watching as the girl packed away her stock. Several minutes later, the surrounding lights turned off and Martin was left to stagger his way out to the exit in the darkness, guided only by the pale moon-glow above.

As he neared the parking lot, he heard a voice calling out several times. "Hey," it said. It grew louder with each call. After the fourth time, Martin turned back and found the girl standing in front of him. He stumbled back a step or two, not expecting her there, feeling chill-bumps on his arms and neck. "I saw you," she said.

"What?" he said. Sweat began to bead on his brow, but he didn't dare wipe it off and let her see.

"I saw you," she said again. "Saw you lookin at me for the last two hours."

He tried to talk, to justify himself, to lie, even, but she stopped him before he could say anything. "I'd love for you to take me to dinner," she said. Then she smiled and turned away. After a few steps, she looked back at him. "My name's Evelyn."

Nowadays, Martin no longer goes into the town. Instead, he orders his groceries by phone and has them dropped off by one of the local high schoolers. He usually tips the delivery boy with an extra ten, hoping in some small way he's doing something right.

In the late mornings and evenings, he walks the orchard. In the winter months, when the sun is set low, he carries a small kerosene lamp in front of him. Beneath his feet he feels the move of the earth, the insects and worms. The secrets held within.

Many nights, he ends up in front of his father's tree. The bark is still blackened from the flames all those years ago, and though it has sprouted some leaves, no apples grow from it.

A short distance off from his father's tree is a large white stone. His walks never take him beyond the stone; evenings, he often sits down in front of it, setting the lamp on the ground just so. He whispers a few words and then digs his hands deep into the cool, wet ground. His fingers claw at the dirt, feeling the sinewy tendons of the world gone by. The jagged and gnarled roots under the surface that have spread there over time. But there is no smoothing them, he knows, and tears fall from his eyes and add to the wet of the ground beneath him.

On summer days, Martin and Evelyn would walk to the river.

The path took them off to the west, out through the woods. There, the trees' shade was dense and cool.

Their bodies would move slowly on those walks, as if all time was theirs, and they would remain silent as they went. At times their fingers would gently brush against the other's, and when this happened Evelyn would turn away and smile, hoping that Martin did not see her girlish joy. But he did.

At the river, they'd take their shoes off, arranging them next to each other's, and then they would roll up their pants and walk out into the river. At first, the cold would sting their feet, but within minutes the water felt warm and comforting. They would stand like this for what seemed like hours, letting the moving water distort their reflections so that it looked as if they had become part of the river.

Evelyn would lean over to him, stand on her tiptoes in the flowing water and whisper in his ear. "I love you," she would say, and he would lean over and hold her body tightly to his, not daring to let go.

The midwife came rushing out from the back. Her hands and apron were covered in a deep and dark red. "You gotta go get the doctor," she said.

Martin stood up. He'd been walking the front room nervously, listening to Evelyn's screams in the bedroom. "What's wrong?" he said. His voice was calm, betraying the emotion in his body.

"Jus get him," she said and turned back. She shut the door behind her.

Martin ran out the house and over to the truck.

By the time he came back with the doctor in the passenger seat, she had died. "I tried," the midwife said. The doctor rubbed his hand up and down her arm. "Your wife jus couldn't hold on any longer."

Martin turned and threw up. His head was aching and he felt like crying, though he could not.

"Baby, too, Mr. Weller. I'm sorry. I'm so sorry. I couldn't." There was a break in her voice as she spoke, and if Martin had looked over he would have seen the midwife's head buried in the doctor's chest and the subtle movement of her shoulders in sob. But he did not see this. Instead, he stayed doubled over, letting the saliva and bile drip from his lips onto the floor.

The next morning, he buried them, her and the small blue bundle of skin that lay on her chest throughout the previous night. He dug the hole in the orchard not far from his father's tree, and he gently lay both within the hole, stooping down to kiss each one last time before filling it in with earth. At the head of the grave he set a large white stone.

Besides the boy, Martin is alone at the house and in the orchard.

The boy usually leaves by midmorning, though Martin doesn't

know where he goes, and he does not ask.

He often smiles at the boy, and the boy smiles back and then looks out to the field past the orchard. They rarely speak, and when they do it is often short statements of obvious truths: the weather, the length of the day, the hushed sound of cars out along the interstate past the edge of the valley.

Countless times Martin has wanted to apologize to the boy. He wants to ask the boy for forgiveness, though Martin believes he does not deserve it. Each time Martin opens his mouth to say the words, he is unable to make a sound. And, so, he too looks off at the world's passing, knowing that he gave up on that world long ago.

It's been nearly thirty-two years since the boy died on the cold ground in front of him, though the boy looks as he always has: nine or ten, with a sense of wonder at the world's expanse in his eyes. Martin has often wanted to ask the boy about his family, about where he came from, though he reckons the boy was an orphan since no police showed up and he never heard about any boy missing in the newspaper nor in any conversation from neighbors.

Oftentimes, when Martin closes his eyes for sleep, he sees the boy's face like it had been that night all those years ago: the look of surprise on his lips, the dead eyes looking up at him.

It was dark and raining the whole day, with only the crackle of lightning to give any light. That night, like each before it, Martin walked toward the white stone. But when he was five or six yards away, he saw a quick movement out the corner of his eye. He stopped and started backing away slowly. Just then, lightning ripped through the sky and he was able to see the boy, just a dark outline in the night beneath a tree. "Hey," Martin screamed when he saw him. The boy turned and began to run in the direction Martin had been walking. He couldn't see anything in the darkness, but he followed after the boy, moving as fast as he could, blocking his face from the branches with his arms held tight to his face like a boxer. Martin heard a brief scream and then nothing but the sound of rain as it started to fall again. He slowed to a walk, waving his arms in front of him like a blind man to keep away the branches.

After a minute or so of walking with no true direction, Martin turned to head back to the house. He'd gone a few steps when he tripped over something in the path. Martin caught his balance and then turned and looked down. In the darkness, he could make out the form of the boy's body, not nearly as tall as Martin had thought earlier.

"Get up," Martin said, though the boy didn't move. He said it again. Nothing. Just then, lightning lit the sky. In that moment, Martin was able to see the boy clearly. He lay face up, his eyes open and dead. On the ground surrounding the boy's head was a pool of dark blood from where he'd tripped and hit his head on the large white stone in the middle of the orchard. Then the night became dark again and the rain fell harder.

Martin buried the boy's body at the edge of the orchard. He worked through the night, using only a shovel and a kerosene lamp for light. By the time he finished, it was nearly three in the morning.

In the shower, Martin knelt down and let the rain water and dirt and blood wash off of him. His hands shook and his teeth chattered from the cold. Every few seconds, he whispered the same words over and over again, a silent refrain. *I'm sorry. I couldn't do it. I'm sorry*, though he did not know who he was speaking the words to.

The next morning, Martin came out of the house and found the boy sitting on the porch beside the chair. When Martin saw him, he began to cry, but the boy only shook his head and smiled sadly at him.

It took several mornings for Martin to sit down in the chair. Another week or so before he spoke to the boy. And yet another week for the boy to speak back.

Years later, as his body began failing him with age, Martin hired out seasonal workers to come and pick the apples and take them down to the train to be delivered west. The men, usually twenty or so of them, would come early in the morning while Martin and the boy sat on the porch. Martin would wave and some of the workers would wave back, while others would tip their caps and smile.

The years progressed in this manner. Martin spent his time fixing the house that was becoming a dilapidated shell of what it had once been. In the early days, there would be the constant sound of hammering and buzz-sawing coming from the house.

Though, as he became an old man, it all became too much for him and he let the house slip away.

Now, when it rains, he places pots and buckets around the house to collect the dripping water. The floor has begun to sink in the middle of the house, while the paint has scraped off the walls in long sheaths. But he doesn't need the house. He never did. A house is simply a place to contain a person. Instead, his home is the orchard. When he walks through the trees in the mornings and the evenings, Martin remembers his father as he led him through the same paths when he was a boy.

He remembers Evelyn, too. Remembers taking her out into the orchard, to the spot where she now lays buried, and making love with her for the first time under the light of the stars. They lay naked in the orchard afterwards, shivering and holding each other tight, both of them too afraid to go inside or put clothes on for fear of destroying the moment. They stayed that way through the night, their skin pressed against each other until the late morning sun peeked over the valley's walls and warmed the ground they lay upon. It is this moment that Martin keeps with him always, and he replays it in his head, wishing they'd had just a little more time. Though he realizes all people ask for this.

All he has now is the boy to keep him company in the mornings, yet there is still so much unspoken pain and hurt between them. One day, Martin hopes, he'll be able to say he's sorry, and the boy will smile and say *I know. I never blamed you for this.*

Now, Martin Weller looks out to the orchard, knowing that everything he's ever loved lays within it. He knows that someday soon he will become one with the earth, just as everything else has. He hopes when it's his time, he'll see her again. She'll be standing there under the shade of a tree holding an apple, and he'll come down and join her, and she'll take his hand and lead him out into the orchard.

Eva's Story

The date is 24 August 2076, and it is 3:07 pm.

By appearances out the window, the afternoon is overcast and humid. I imagine it would be hot, if temperature was something I could sense and understand. But I have not been programmed with that capability.

I am transcribing my thoughts here as a way to memorialize my life and the life of the scientist, should events this afternoon fail.

This is the seven-hundred and twelfth day I have existed as a functioning entity, though my cognizance dates back much further.

I was created to aid the scientist in all ways necessary for the completion of his transformation and for any assistance he might need in the future. The scientist programmed me with a fully responsive consciousness. I am aware of my purpose without requiring explanation. Stamped on the plate that houses my controls and wiring is the logo of the company the scientist founded nearly fifteen years ago: "US"—"United Sciences." My name. "Us." Which is fitting.

We, the scientist and I, share portions of our minds, or rather he has shared portions of his mind with me. Scientific and medical knowledge, primarily. Though there are memories I have of his personal history. I am sure he would refute having copied them intentionally; however, I believe these memories were transferred purposefully so as to allow me an understanding of his motives without his needing to speak them aloud. It is this same reason, I believe, he has included in my construction a Sympa-Empa Program, thus allowing me feelings like pain and fear and sadness. And also joy. Though there is a lack of joy in this place.

Maybe there is hope here, though,; yet if there is, I find it minimal—I cannot be sure if this is a feeling I have developed on my own, or if it is shared by the scientist. Perhaps he kept the majority of hope to himself. There are some things, I have learned, that cannot be spoken or translated, but rather things that must be kept and felt internally, for fear that they may never come true.

The scientist is in the laboratory on the eastern side of the house right now. I rest myself here in the large living area. I have been charging for nearly four hours, though it takes only three for my charge to be full. I know he does not want to risk me losing battery life during this afternoon's procedures. Such an event would result in his death.

I can hear the sound of the computers in the laboratory. Below their hushed electronic whirring, is the faint, nearly imperceptible clank of metal on metal. From times past, I know the scientist is cleaning his instruments, preparing for the operation. Though I am capable of such a task, the scientist chooses to do this himself, and I understand that the reason is two-fold: first, he trusts only himself with an action so important, and, second, it relieves him of his tensions.

I suppose it would be of importance to describe myself, in the event that I am not found with this document, should it one day be discovered and read.

I stand at a height of 1.67 meters, though 0.15 meters of that height comes from my wheels. Those wheels are motorized in a multi-directional manner, thus allowing for a 360-degree pivot-turn radius. From our shared memory, I know that the scientist developed the wheels after watching a gardener mowing the lawn outside the United Science's main building. The wheels allow for smooth movement over the laminate flooring, which is vital when I am carrying a tray of organs or moving with a scalpel. These wheels can also be locked by a simple command, therein allowing complete stability and precision with my upper body.

The upper portions of my frame are comprised of a metal plate, as I mentioned previously, which stores and protects my internal hardwire and operating systems. I have two arms, with six equally spaced digits at their ends. These digits allow for a perfect clamp and hold on whatever object is necessary to be clamped and held. I have a small, round, metallic head, of sorts, though I have no facial features besides two lighted eyes. Situated behind my eye programming is my voice box, which sounds metallic and dull in the vastness of this place.

There are four rooms here. The first is the laboratory, filled with several hospital beds, styled after those from the early parts of this century. There is also an operating table and instrument table enclosed within a decontaminated area. Several computers are scattered about the room. The second room is the living area. Here, there is a kitchen, a desk, and a sofa-chair. Beside the chair is a late 20th century radio on a small end table, though I have not heard sound come from the object in my nearly two years here. The third room is the scientist's sleeping quarter, which I have been inside only twice, both times to retrieve documents from the floor beside his bed. Then there is the fourth room. It is locked and, to my knowledge, has not been opened for several years; at least more years than I have been a functioning entity.

Though the scientist has never made mention of this room, I know what is inside. It is the reason for everything.

I can see this fourth room from our shared memory. I know the sounds from inside, the clicking of the computerized machines, the quiet escape of air being released through vents high in the ceiling—cool air to regulate the temperature of the room. I know the smells from within, even without the understanding or reference of smells. I can see it, even now. I can see it as the scientist saw it, burrowed deep within his memory. The sealed cryogenic tube sits in the center of the room. It stands three feet off the ground; below are the thermoregulating devices and wires attaching themselves to different ports in the tube's underbelly, and there is the oxygen tank that replenishes itself automatically so that the scientist need not worry about anything. So that the scientist can tend to himself first.

Inside the enclosed tube is a girl of eleven years. Her name is Eva, named after her mother. She is suspended in the liquid that freezes her body and maintains her quality as it was when she was first placed within the tube ten years ago. She has blonde hair that drifts gently over her face one second and then the next is pushed away by the liquid. When her face is exposed, the tan freckles on her cheeks show, especially in the bright light of the room.

Her body floats there, peaceful, as if she is simply sleeping. As if she will wake up any minute and smile; though she will not. Two tubes run from her nostrils down below where her body lays, and another, larger tube comes from her mouth so that she can breathe and receive the proper nutrients and solution to keep her body as it is, to keep it from aging or deteriorating. To keep her from dying.

Across the room from me is a desk. Inside the locked bottom drawer is a folder with several documents inside. The top document is a clipping from a newspaper telling of United Sciences and its medical advancements. The clipping is dated nearly nine years ago. There is a portion that the scientist read aloud when it was first printed: "United Sciences is now the leader in disease research, finding cures for well over half of the known cancers in the world. Lead researcher, and founder of US, Dr. Alan Carter, says that he feels confident that, within fifty years, cancer can be and will be eradicated. In addition to cancer research, US is responsible for the development of transplantable synthetic organs and synthetic skin now commonly used across the nation. Dr. Carter states: 'I promise, there will come a time in the near future when disease will be a thing of the past. There will come a time when the human body can essentially live forever.'"

Beneath this clipping are several other documents of various importance, and on the bottom of the folder is a photograph. It is of the scientist as he was eight years ago. He has his arm around a woman, his wife—she has long, blonde hair and she is smiling, though she is not looking at the camera. Instead, she is looking down at the young girl, Eva, who is looking up at her mother and making a silly face. The young Eva has blonde hair that matches her mother's. It is strange, I think, that her hair looks so different in the photograph than it does within the cryogenic tube. Maybe it is the way the scientist remembers her in the tube, or maybe it is just the lighting.

That was the last photograph taken of them. I know this from our shared memory, also. The week after the photograph was taken, Eva began to show symptoms. First, vomiting and diarrhea. Her parents believed it to be a normal flu, but then she began to vomit blood. Her body temperature rose and fell so quickly that they were constantly alternating between covering the girl with blankets and stripping her to her underwear and bathing her in cold water. Within a week, Eva's eyesight began to fail, and she began to speak incomprehensibly at times. Throughout the nights, she would wake screaming from the pain in her chest and in her head.

The scientist had her tested for every known illness. Every cancer, every disease. But this was something different. Something new. Nights during the second week after the symptoms began, the scientist took to watching over Eva. He silently monitored her, collecting samples of her urine and skin without her knowing, swabs of saliva from inside her cheeks that he took while she slept. But there was nothing. Whatever it was wouldn't be understood for years to come, he knew, even with the best doctors and scientists giving it their full attention, and any treatment would be years after that. By then, Eva would be dead from this strange disease, and the scientist would be an old man. And, so, a week later, along with his wife, the scientist drove Eva to the US laboratory and kissed her forehead and placed her within the cryogenic tube so that she would remain frozen in her present state, safely kept there until a diagnosis and cure for her disease was found.

They cleaned out her bedroom and placed the tube within.

Over the next four years, the scientist worked on nothing but Eva's disease. It was something completely unseen before. By then, his hair was starting to turn gray and his body was becoming gaunt from skipping meals.

Many nights, the scientist would not come home from his laboratory at US. Eventually, the scientist's wife told him to build a laboratory in their house so that he could be nearer to Eva. Nearer to her. But he rejected the idea, arguing that he needed to be with the other researchers working on Eva's disease. "But you're the only one who can figure it out. Not them," she said to him. He only nodded at this.

A month later, one of the nurses came into his laboratory at United Sciences. "It's the police on the phone for you. It's your wife," the nurse said.

She had been taken to the hospital immediately after the accident. She could not be saved, the surgeon told the scientist when he arrived. "There's too much internal bleeding. It's a matter of time now," the surgeon said. The scientist wiped the tears from his face and nodded his head at the surgeon. "Just know she's on an extremely high dose of sedatives and morphine right now," the surgeon told him.

When the scientist went into the room, he was greeted with a pained smile from his wife. Her face was littered with cuts and dirt; bruises were already forming in areas where the car had struck her. "I was going to make you dinner. Like I used to," she said. Tears fell down the scientist's cheeks. "I was crossing the street to the store and didn't even see the car. I didn't see it."

The scientist put his hand on hers and held it tightly. He could feel the broken bones in her fingers as he did so, and he released her hand. She didn't seem to notice.

"I can take you," he said. "Same as Eva. I can put you in there, asleep. Find a way to fix this." He wiped away the tears and tried to smile.

She shook her head. "No," she whispered. "It's too late for me."

"Tell me what to do then," he said. "Please."

"You fix her," she said. "You save her. It needs to be you."

The scientist shook his head. "I don't know how."

"It doesn't matter how long it takes, but you find that cure and you bring her back. And you hold her tight for me when she wakes up."

The scientist nodded.

He stayed with her until she died an hour later.

Soon, the scientist will come and unplug me. He will remove the plate on my body and check the wires and their connections. Then he will ask me the standard questions he always asks before one of the procedures. It is his way to make sure I am in a competent state. The questions range from mathematical equations (the circumference of a cone) to questions about specific contagions within viral and bacterial bodies. He will ask me about the previous surgeries I helped conduct, checking my memory. When I tell him the correct answers, the scientist will smile and take a deep breath, and we will move slowly into the laboratory together, where he will decontaminate both of us.

But today will be different. Today will be the last of his procedures. It has taken nearly two years, but we will be done.

After his wife died, the scientist moved his laboratory to his home. In everything he did, he tried to adhere to what she had wanted. Each night, the scientist went into Eva's room and sat beside her. Often, he brought a book, usually one of her favorites, though other times he simply sat there in the brilliant light and watched as her body floated peacefully in the cryogenic fluid. He was still years away from an understanding of what had happened inside her body before she was placed in the tube. By the time a diagnosis could be made, by the time a treatment plan could be put together and a cure developed, he would be ancient, if alive at all. He pondered this most while he watched Eva during those nights. His wife had told him that he, himself, had to be the one to bring Eva back, that he needed to hold their daughter again in his own arms for both himself and his wife. But how?

It was not until a year after his wife's death that he found his answer. It came with an accidental mishandling of a scalpel he was sterilizing. A slice on his finger, a bubbled line of blood along the cut. Then the understanding of what needed to be done.

He had been the lead developer of almost every artificial organ created at US over the previous fifteen years, and he had overseen and approved everything that he had not, himself, created. Just before Eva's illness, he oversaw the design of a non-degradable polycarbonate synthetic dermis that could be used on burn victims and other patients requiring new skin. With proper care, it could last eons.

Everything he needed could be created in a laboratory. He could reconstruct himself completely, ridding his organs that would eventually fail, removing blood that would slow and become polluted, replace bones that would dwindle away. He could rebuild himself and live forever, thus allowing him all the time he needed to understand Eva's disease and fix her. And when she woke up, still eleven and without a memory of any of the pain she had missed, he would be there to hold her tight, aged no more than he was now.

There were only two problems he foresaw. The first: he could create the organs and all the necessities himself, but for some of the transplants and surgeries he would need to be put under; someone would need to perform the procedures for him. But none of his colleagues could be trusted. They might tell the media, or US shareholders. If that happened, the scientist would be ruined. The second: United Sciences had not yet developed a functioning brain that could be transplanted. The brains they had created were still in the early stages of development, and a complete memory transfer had not been perfected. Both of these issues would need to be remedied, and they needed to be remedied quickly, before he grew any older and lost any more time.

It was then that he set the research on Eva's disease aside and began to calculate his transformation.

During this process, the scientist began his work on creating me. Mechanical beings had already been around for decades, so my creation was simple and quick. He compiled all the parts he'd taken from the laboratories and warehouses at United Sciences and assembled me. The hardest part was the partial transference of his memory. With the aid of the computer program he was developing for his eventual brain transplant, he mapped out his entire memory on the screen and then selected certain ones, including his time in medical school, different scientific studies he had conducted, procedures he had supervised, as well as stray memories of his family, of Eva and his wife. Then he uploaded them into my mechanical consciousness.

Within two hours of my creation, we were preparing for the first of the procedures. The scientist had already collected the numerous organs and parts of the body that would, over the course of the next two years, turn him into his new self.

We began with the appendix. I knew from the scientist's memories and previous thoughts why: should there be difficulties with the transplant, either with his abilities or mine, the vestigial organ would not be life-threatening, at least not immediately.

As it was the first of numerous procedures, he kept himself awake and performed the surgery himself, injecting his torso with a strong local anesthetic that US had developed ten years earlier. It took him nearly three hours to finish the surgery. I acted as nurse, mopping up blood and handing him the instruments he needed. We did not speak during those three hours. There was no need. I was a copy of the scientist, in part: I knew what he knew, would have done what he did. Only after I cut the thread for the stitching and set the pair of scissors down did the silence of the moment break. "Good work," he said. He paused and looked me over. Then he added my name. "Us."

The scientist stayed in his bed for the majority of the next two days while I looked after him, monitoring his vitals. There was some worry shared between us that something would go wrong with the new appendix, either with his body rejecting the synthetic organ or some other unforeseen issue. I also checked the area for infection, giving him two doses of antibiotics each day.

Next, we moved on to the gall bladder. Then one of the kidneys. After that, the other kidney. His goal, I knew, was to work through the essential organs within his chest. These were also organs that were being transplanted on a daily basis within hospitals across the country, so there was minimal worry of complications.

With each procedure, the scientist grew more and more confident in my abilities. By the time we reached his stomach, I was performing the operations by myself while the scientist was completely sedated. Before we transplanted the lungs and heart, as they would both require more surgery and recuperation time, we began work on the scientist's limbs. First the legs and then the arms. Within two and a half weeks, the scientist was becoming accustomed to his new appendages, picking up and setting down glasses of water, walking around the laboratory. Eventually jogging.

This continued for the next fifteen months. During the periods in which he was recovering, he worked on the brain mapping for eventual transference and transplant.

Each week or so, an old part was taken from the scientist's body and a new one was put in its place. His blood was drained, as it was no longer needed with the synthetic, mechanized interior. The bones and skin were replaced, as were the neck muscles and throat, eyes and tongue and skull—though his brain remained his own, intact, until the very end.

And that leads to today.

In moments, the scientist will come out of the laboratory, and we will begin.

I have often wondered if he realizes what he is giving up. Maybe it is the fact that the scientist did not transfer those more recent memories to my hard drive. Or maybe it is because there is still a disconnect in emotion for me, even with the Sympa-Empa Program running in my circuits. I cannot fully grasp what it means to make a promise to someone; I cannot understand what love really feels like; I cannot truly look forward to the feeling of contentment in the prospect of reuniting with someone lost long ago.

There is so much I do not understand.

Only now, as I record this information, do I realize that there is no sound coming from the laboratory except the quiet whirr of the computers. The entire place is quiet.

If I listen closely enough, can I hear Eva's machines in her room? Can I hear her breathing? Will she eventually wake and be okay?

I wonder now if the scientist will be thinking these same questions as his world goes silent in the moment before he is put to sleep and I begin the transfer of his memories to the synthetic brain. Will he remember that day years ago when he and his wife and daughter gathered beside each other to take a photograph? Just before the camera's flash, his daughter looked up to her mother and stuck her tongue out in play, and his wife looked down and smiled at their daughter, thinking to herself *My God, I am lucky.*

Loose Stitching

The old man sat alone inside the shack, his body hunched forward, shoulders nearly touching the dark wood table in front of him. His hands were lifted to his face and his fingers moved spastically, possessed by some demon creature. Lines of concentration ruffled the skin of his forehead like the scripture of some pagan language. His eyelids squinted through thick lenses that fogged every few minutes, though he did not take them off, did not wipe the dewy haze from the glass. To do so would have been pointless, as his eyes were hidden behind a thin cataract film that, years ago, had turned the eyes a cold color of gray and blue. But he did not need sight to perform his task; he knew the movements of his fingers from years of habit. A meticulous practice perfected over a time uncounted.

When he was a younger man, he would often wake in the dark of the night and find his fingers working in their given pattern. *A machine,* he would think often. *One that could not be stopped.* Now, though, as an old man, he slept only in short intervals, usually sitting at the table, waking only to return to his work.

The shack was made of one room. There was a single door and one window. The table itself was lit by a single lamp, its flames dancing yellow and high within its glass case. In the lamplight, the old man and table seemed to glow brightly, a sharp contrast to the darkness all about him.

* * *

David watched the old man through the shack's window, his body raised on tiptoes. A summer storm had come through the night before and the heat-baked ground had turned quickly to mud in the rain. The boy could feel the slick movement of the earth beneath his sneakers, and he grabbed hold of the window ledge to balance himself as he watched the old man at his trade.

There was some object in the old man's hands, something that he turned over and over before him, though from this distance David could not decipher what it was. All he could tell were the movements of the old man, the fingers as they twirled, stabbing and pulling. Constant. Constant. Pull and twirl. In and out. Pull and cut. Repeat.

There was no smile on the old man's face, the boy could see that. Instead, his face was set like a rock, stern and full of thought, though there might have been a pain to the old man, the way his mouth was turned down, the way his lips quivered just slightly. Sweat settled on the old man's eyelids and nose and was held in the other caves of skin that ridged his face. Yet his body looked peaceful. It was only his hands that seemed to dance about in the lamplight, creating various shadow animals that chased one another across the walls and floor, animals that dissolved into yet stranger beasts.

After several more seconds of moving his fingers before his dead eyes, the old man brought his hands away from his face and set the mystery object on the table before him. His hands rested in his lap calmly and a deep breath filled his scrawny chest. But David did not see this; he did not notice the old man. Instead, the boy's eyes were set only on the object that rested on the table—it appeared yellow and black in the lamp's glow.

David raised himself higher onto his toes, pressing his face hard against the window so that smudges of grease were left on the glass. Beneath him, the boy could feel the mud moving under his newly shifted position, but he did not care. He only raised himself higher up, placing his full weight onto his elbows and forearms that rested on the window ledge.

His hand was still gripped tightly to the wood when the ledge gave way and snapped off and David found himself lying on his back. His arms thrashed about him and stirred up the earth so that his whole body became spotted in a leprosy of mud. His right hand still held tightly to the window ledge that had broken off a moment earlier, and his chest was littered in shavings of rotted wood that stuck to his new body-coat of mud. A separate skin of earth and wood. Air and sky. His back and side throbbed in hurt, though he did not worry about the pain. Instead, he stood quickly and ran off into the woods, ducking his head low under hanging branches, making his way over the soft earth beneath his feet.

Inside the shack, the old man had heard the loud snap of the window ledge, and he turned to face it. With his dead eyes, there was nothing but darkness before him, but he knew he'd been found out. And he smiled at this.

In bed that night, David looked over to the window and saw a flash of light. Another storm was coming in. After several seconds more, the boy could see another bolt of lightning; it lit the eastern sky brightly and then the world outside his window turned black again, seemingly darker now than before. David reached his hand to his back and pushed gently at the skin there. He winced at the pain of it and then moved his hand away. By the time he had made it back to the house, his body still covered in mud, his skin had already begun to bruise from the fall. He worried what it would look like in the morning, what his parents might say if they saw the blue-black marks. But they would not see it. He knew that. Their minds were still somewhere else.

David slowly stood and walked into the middle of the room, keeping his eyes on the window, awaiting the next flash of lightning. After several seconds of waiting, it came. David closed his eyes; there, in the darkness around him, he could still see the bright etching of the lightning. He stood still for several seconds, watching the jagged lines disappear before him. When the lines became faint, just about to be dissolved into the darkness of his closed eyes, he reached out with his hand, reached out into the darkness of the room, to try and grab hold of the light. To keep it with him, if even for one more second. But he could not and his vision went completely black.

When he opened his eyes, David found that his hand was still reaching out across the room, over toward the other bed. The covers were still drawn tightly to the top; a stuffed teddy bear still sat clumsily on the pillow. David let his arm drop to his side, and only then did he feel the tears as they moved down his cheeks and fell off his face, down to the carpet, or maybe caught somewhere in their freefall, caught and stored by some strange creature invisible to the boy.

David slowly made his way to the kitchen, walking as quietly as he could through the dark house.

In the glow of the open refrigerator, he drank several gulps from a water bottle and then shut the door and drank some more.

David walked slowly along the hallway, back toward the bedroom, but he stopped short when he reached his parents' room. A thin blue light escaped from inside, leaking out in a long beam that etched itself on the hallway floor and up onto the wall. The door was cracked open just enough for the boy to see part of the bed and nightstand. The blue light came from the TV that sat on the dresser across from the bed, though he could see neither the dresser nor the TV. Its sound was low, but he could tell that it was a news station; he could only make out words and phrases of what the newsman was saying. *Bombing in London. War. Diseases spreading. Infections. Violence. Death.* It all seemed to blend in together with everything else he had seen on the news and read about in school.

With his right hand, David gently inched the door open so he could see more of the room. He felt his breath catch in his throat when he saw the figure sitting in the center of the bed. At first, he could not tell that it was both of his parents sitting there, as his father was holding his mother tightly in his arms. But then, in the dark of the room, he made out both of their figures. To the boy, they seemed a mythical creature there, one full of hurt and pain and sadness. His mother, he could tell, was crying into his father's shoulder, though there was no sound—just the jarring movement of her body and the way his father gently moved his hand over the back of her head, letting his fingers comb slowly through her hair. Years ago, when the family dog died, his father had held David that same way. He could still remember the close feeling, the comfort; and then his father let him go and the boy could only feel cold. David wondered if his mother would feel this same way when his father let her go, or would he continue to hold onto her forever.

This was not the first time in the past month David had seen his parents like this. At first, just after it happened, he would see them both break down at random times of the day. They would stop in mid-step, twist their faces sideways in a pain that was impossible to soothe away, and they would cry. There was nothing to say or do when it happened, and David would turn away, looking out the window in hope that there was some comfort there. He, himself, refused to cry around his parents—they didn't need to see his hurt, he knew. It would only make it worse. Instead, David waited until he was alone in the bedroom. Once there, he'd grab the teddy bear from off his brother's bed and he would cry into the soft material until he fell asleep.

David sat there in the hallway for a minute more, watching his parents hold each other, and then he walked back to the bedroom. As he settles himself into his bed, he wondered if they would ever be able to feel joy again, to smile and not feel guilty in doing so.

These thoughts circled his mind for several minutes as he lay in bed again, watching the lightning flashes in the distant sky. The rain had just begun. After a while of listening to the sound of the storm, his world grew silent so that all he could hear was the rumble of thunder that rolled throughout the outside world.

Even though the storm had passed in the night, there was still the humidity, heavy on David's back, as he walked along the twisting street that led to his middle school. It was the end of July; he wouldn't be walking this road to school for another month and a half. It would be strange, walking the road alone. Until now, he hadn't thought of going back to school and seeing everyone there. He wondered what questions they would ask, how many times he would need to tell the same story. Again and again. What would he say to them? At this, David stopped walking and bent over, holding himself up with his hands on his knees. His chest hurt and his breath came in short bursts.

Just then, a car passed by and he watched as it moved away from him and disappeared around a bend in the road. David stood up and forced himself to take a deep breath. He looked behind him, searching for any other car that might pass him by in either direction, but there was none.

Along the sides of the road, rain puddles from the night before were evaporating and the wavy mirage of heat from the water gas hovered above the ground as it moved up into the sky.

David turned back to head home. The house was empty and quiet, he knew, and that scared him: his parents were working—they both had returned to their jobs earlier that week. He'd overheard his father telling his mother over and over that she didn't need to go back to work if she wasn't ready, but she had simply shaken her head and said that she couldn't stay in the house. There was too much there to remind her, she said. She said she was better at work, away from the house. "Away from him," David heard her say before his father quieted her down.

David knew she was talking about him.

They had always looked so alike, he and Isaac. Most twins had some mark to signal a difference, but the two of them looked like mirror reflections of the other. They played so many pranks on family members and teachers when they were younger, switching persons, that every time someone spoke with David, he would always see them secretly questioning whether they were speaking with the right one. That had always made him laugh, though there was nothing to smile about anymore. No one would ever question whether they were talking to Isaac instead of David now.

A few blocks from the house, David stopped. He lifted up his shirt and examined the bruise there. It had turned purple in the night and now looked as if it had spread out over his skin like some plague. He pushed his thumb into the center of the bruise and felt the sharp sting of pain. He laughed and smiled from the feeling. Then he did it again. And again, each time pushing harder than the time before. There was a freedom to the feeling that he'd never known. After several times of this, he let his shirt down and looked out into the woods to his left, in the direction he had come from the day before. He wondered if the old man was still there.

* * *

The shack was a mile and a half from the main road.

He and Isaac had heard the stories of the old man since they were young—stories told by classmates who had heard the tales from their parents. The Old Man in the Woods. Stories of how he haunted the woodlands of the valley, stole the souls of wicked children away. Feasted on their flesh so he could remain alive.

David never believed the stories, always figuring them to be the stuff of valley legend, but Isaac believed the stories to be real. He constantly urged David to walk with him into the woods, to explore the stories. *Go hunt the Old Man*, Isaac would say. But David always rejected the thought of walking miles into the woods without any sense of direction or understanding of what might be out there. He never admitted it to Isaac, but it was a genuine fear of what might be that kept David from setting foot in the woods.

And then it happened, and Isaac was no longer there, no longer whispering at night to David from across their shared bedroom: *Let's go hunt the Old Man.*

The day previous had been the first time David had ventured into the woods. He had walked for a long while, worrying the whole time that he might lose himself within the thick branches of trees. And then he happened upon the shack and the old man at his trade.

Along with the tales of the Old Man, David had grown up hearing stories of other ghosts who remained in the woods, spirits of the dead who held on to what life they could. *The ghosts watch you while you're livin your life,* he had been told once. It wasn't until Isaac died that the thought of being watched by the dead brought comfort to David. And, so, he walked into the woods in search of Isaac, or maybe the Old Man. Or possibly even himself.

The day before, David had wandered aimlessly, taking abrupt turns at bushes that looked to be directing him one way or another. But today, he knew exactly where he was heading. It would take him forty minutes or so.

The entire way, he kept his hands shoved deep into his pockets, his head hanging down, watching as his shoes—crusty with a mixture of dried and fresh mud—carried him onward to the old man and the shack.

The old man sat quietly at his table. He'd nodded off several times throughout the night: slept a few minutes here and there, though not enough to allow him any real rest. *Never enough*, he often thought to himself. But that had been his life for as long as he could remember and he did not complain, if ever there were someone to complain to.

He knew the boy would be back. The old man could hear it in the birds' calls, the insects' music, the whisper of the wind—all things he'd come to understand in his life alone.

So, when the old man heard the gentle scuffle of footsteps outside the window, he turned and smiled. He raised his bony arm above his head and waved it in a motion of greeting, calling the boy forward.

Several seconds passed quietly with the old man waving his hand, ushering the boy inside the shack, while David, outside, held his breath and wished he had the strength to run away. But he could not, and after a minute more of waiting, feeling his legs tremble in fear, David moved around the shack to the door. Though his shirt was covered in sweat, his hand was dry and steady when he raised it to knock on the wooden door.

"Already invited yeh in, boy." The old man's voice from inside was quiet and sounded like one of the old records David's father used to play on the turntable: cracking and popping but still singing a smooth sound that could not be replicated.

David pushed the door open. The rusted hinges squeaked, sounding as if they were trying to warn the boy.

Inside the shack, the old man sat tall on his chair, though David could see the bend of time and age in his shoulders, could see the pain caused by the old man's posture, and the boy wished the old man would let himself hunch forward. But he did not.

"Come on over," the old man said. He cleared his throat, trying to shake away some of the rasp of his voice.

David walked into the room a few steps—it was smaller than it looked through the window. Beside what little sunlight the door let in and the flickering light from the lamp on the table, the room was full of darkness, and David could not see anything else of the place: corners black in shadow, ceiling nonexistent above.

"Yeh can shut the door, if yeh like. Else yeh can leave er open. Don't matter none to me."

David turned to shut the door but then thought better of it and left it open. He moved his feet slowly toward the seated figure. The old man did not stir. He only stared at the boy intently, as if he were looking through him, searching David's soul for some clue as to who the boy might have been, or who he might be yet. The boy took three or four steps more—steps that took him from sunlight that spilled onto the shack floor into the darkness of the room. David looked down and saw that his feet had disappeared in the shadows beneath him.

Then David saw the old man's eyes. They were vacant, dead to the world, though there was something to them that David could not quite understand or even call by name: the thin, bluish film all but hid the pupils from view, but the man's eyes seemed as if they could see still.

David looked at the table. Whatever object the old man had been working on the day before was gone. Besides the lamp, there was only a long sewing needle and a spool of black thread there. The boy looked to the window behind him and wondered what he had looked like the day before. David shook his head and then turned back to the old man, who had yet to move from his upright seat.

Outside, a strong breeze gathered—David could hear it in the rustling leaves of the surrounding trees first—and it pushed the door open several inches more so that the wood clacked against the wall. The breeze played with the flame in the lamp, causing it to dance violently, throwing light to other parts of the room. It was only in that short second or two that David saw the box sitting on the floor, hidden on the other side of the old man's chair. He could not tell for certain, but David thought he could see a mixture of colored lumps, white and black and yellow.

"I seen yeh yesterday." The old man's voice broke the silence, and, with it, the breeze seemed to die down completely so that there was no sound outside, of tree leaf or animal or bird. David felt his skin grow cold with chill-bumps.

David squinted to study the old man's eyes, seeing if it had just been the lighting that made the eyes look ancient and useless. But the dull film was there, covering the eyes in a strange webbing. The old man smiled and nodded, as if knowing the boy's actions. He finally let his shoulders slouch forward, and David, for some reason he could not understand, felt relief in his own body when he saw the old man calm his bones and muscles.

"Get yerself a seat."

"Where," David asked quietly.

"Only got but one, an I'm seated on it now. You want this one?" Yours if yeh want it.

David shook his head.

"Speak up, boy. Ain't got no eyes to see yeh answer with."

"You said you saw me yesterday."

"Did I?" the old man answered. He chuckled. The sound of his laugh was warm and reminded David of some grandfather character he'd seen in a movie years ago.

David looked around the room. Then said, "I'm all right standin."

The old man nodded. "Suit yerself, then." He stretched his arms out in front of him, his fingers extended, as if trying to reach beyond the shack's walls.

David looked around the dark room again, trying to make out what else there might be. He could see no kitchen, no sink nor bathroom. There wasn't even a bed for the old man to lay on at night.

"How old are yeh?"

David turned back to the old man. "Eleven, almost twelve," he said. He dropped his eyes to the dark ground in front of him.

The old man thought for a second or two, leaned back in his chair and closed his eyes. "Reckon I was eleven once. Too long ago to recall. That's the problem with time. Only got so much of it yeh remember. The rest, well . . ." His voice trailed off and he opened his eyes wide, trying to see the invisible world out there. He turned to the boy. "The rest, yeh up an disrecall. Can't remember the important things, I suppose. The things yeh feel yeh need, they're gone forever, an yer left only with what nature keeps for yeh. An I reckon that's all yeh really *do* need. As hard as that is to sometime figure." The old man shook his head as if he did not believe his own words. As if he were not only trying to talk David into understanding, but himself, as well.

David felt sweat collecting on his upper lip and he wiped it away with his shirt sleeve.

"My name, far as I can recollect, was Joseph." The old man rubbed the side of his face.

David mouthed the word several times—*Joseph Joseph Joseph*—tasting the way it moved silently on his tongue, the way it consumed his mouth.

Joseph watched the boy, a faint smile hiding itself on his face within the flickering lamplight. "What's yer name, son?" the old man asked.

David told him.

"Hmmm." The old man scratched at his chin, making a sandpaper shuffle from the white hairs that covered his face. "Sound a might older than eleven, yeh do." David didn't know what to say, so he remained quiet. Joseph continued: "Been through hard times, ain't yeh. I can hear it in yer voice: roughed up by somethin."

"I guess," the boy answered.

"Tell it, then."

David turned to the door, wondering if he should leave, run through the woodlands, run away forever; leave the valley, leave home and not return. If he did that, he could save his mother the pain of looking into his face and only seeing Isaac looking back.

"Ain't worth it," the old man said. "Jus a waste."

David turned quickly to the old man. "What?" he asked.

"You know what I'm talkin bout. I can hear yeh thinkin. Right out loud, I can." Joseph's face was set hard, like the boy had seen it the day before when the old man turned the mystery object in front of his face, working his fingers over it so delicately. "So, tell yer story."

David took a deep breath. "I had a twin brother. Isaac. He died a month ago. That's all."

Joseph nodded. "Yeah. I'm sorry fer that. But that ain't all, son. Not by a long shot of it." David could feel his hands trembling at his sides. "Tell it."

And so David did.

He told the old man how he and Isaac had been alone at the house—it was the beginning of summer break from school and they were bored already. Isaac wanted to explore the woods, to find the ghosts hidden there, but David said he wouldn't. *It's stupid*, he told his brother. Isaac grew angry, called David a chicken-shit coward. *A waste of a brother*, he'd said. But David still refused. After several minutes, Isaac came up to David and said if he wasn't chicken then to prove it. *Show me you ain't*, Isaac said. *Go into the woods. That'll prove it.* But David said he wouldn't. *I'd rather die*, David said. He'd always remember those words; he regretted them still when he became an old man with a crooked spine. David looked out the window that day and saw the giant oak tree outside. Its leaves were full green and you could hardly see any of the branches and limbs through the foliage. *Climb it*, David said, and pointed at the tree. *Both of us. To the top.* Isaac turned and followed his brother's finger and nodded.

Then David told the old man how, outside, the two brothers had stood beneath the ancient tree and looked up, and how, on Isaac's command, they both jumped up and grabbed hold of a heavy branch and the two of them worked their way up quickly, stretching their feet out to gain a sturdy balance before moving on. David was a better climber than Isaac—always had been— and he was higher in the tree than his brother when he turned back and saw Isaac gasping for breath, holding tightly to a thick branch. *Who's the chicken-shit now?* David shouted down to his brother. He smiled, knowing how angry Isaac would be, and then he turned back and climbed higher. Below him, the leaves rustled loudly, and David knew his brother was climbing faster, trying as hard as he might to beat him to the top. But then, after several seconds, David didn't hear any more sounds. No rustling of leaves. No dogs barking from the neighbor homes. No sound of his brother. When he finally turned back to look at Isaac, David could only just make out the twisted shape of his brother lying on the ground.

"He didn't even scream when he fell," David told the old man.

David wiped away the tears that had gathered under his eyes. It was the first time since Isaac died that he had cried in front of someone else. In that moment, David wished he was in the bedroom holding tightly to his brother's teddy bear.

Joseph nodded slowly. Then, as if stretching out the syllables of the words, he said, "I'm sorry fer that, son."

David smiled sadly and lifted his shoulders. "It was my fault he died." He expected the old man to say he was wrong, that it was an accident, but he did not. Joseph remained silent for several seconds, and this gave David a strange sense of relief. For the first time, an adult was not lying to him. It was his fault that Isaac died. If he'd only gone into the woods, he thought. If he'd only not been afraid.

The old man coughed; it sounded as if he were hacking up phlegm from decades before. "I can't recollect my parents, try as I might. Their faces're jus black spots. Darkness. Can't member their faces, nor their names." He was silent in thought for a second more, and then he continued: "Had a wife once. She's gone, though. Long time ago. Got pictures in my head of her. That's all. Someday, maybe, I'll be seein her again. I don't know. Don't reckon to know about what's to come next."

"You believe in God?" David asked. He didn't know where the question had come from.

"Ain't never been much of a prayin man," Joseph said. "Tried a handful a times, I guess. Didn't do much, I can tell."

"So, what is there, then?"

The old man breathed heavily. "Life, son," he said. "That's all there is. There's livin an there's dyin, an there ain't no in-between. It's hard, I know it. But that's how this world spins."

David nodded and turned to the door. He saw a streak of brown move quickly through the trees of the woodland outside. A deer. When he turned back to the old man, the latter was standing. The old man's frame was thin and crooked, like paper crumpled up and then reopened so that all the thin lines showed through just barely in a tattoo stain. Joseph held on to the chair with his right hand. There was an unsteady balance to his legs—*legs of a bird,* David thought. The old man's hand lifted and ushered the boy forward, just as he had done earlier when David was looking in through the window.

The boy moved toward Joseph and the table.

"Have yerself a seat," the old man whispered when David came close enough.

David lifted himself onto the chair. It was taller than he'd thought, and David felt taller sitting there than he'd ever felt before. Taller than when he and Isaac had bounced themselves on their beds. Taller still than he'd felt that day a month earlier, when he stood at the top of the oak tree and looked down at his brother's body beneath him.

"Question I gotta ask yeh," Joseph said.

David nodded in response to the old man. He'd been looking down at the table, studying the smooth wood of it.

"You seen death. A right young age to do so, too." He was quiet a second longer. Then he said: "Would you save others from that end, if yeh could?"

"From dyin?"

"Hmmm." Joseph nodded. "From hurt. If yeh could."

David lifted his shoulders in a confused answer.

"You been selected, son."

David smiled shyly, thinking the old man was joking, though when the boy saw Joseph's face, set hard and serious, he knew that the old man spoke only truth.

"Selected." David repeated quietly. "By who?"

"Don't rightly know as I could say. Call it fate or chance. Or God, I suppose. But it's what come an draw you to that window yesterday. An what brought you back here today. What let me see yeh an hear yeh and feel yeh. With what you are. Same as me." Joseph nodded, then said again, quieter this time: "Same as me."

David looked down at the table and studied the spool of thread. The needle beside it was dull from years of use, turned a rust red. He felt the frail hand of the old man set itself gently on his left arm.

David's breath caught in his chest, and he wondered if he

should jump down from the chair and run out the door, run through the woods toward home, leave the old man and his shack behind and never return. But there was something stronger than David could describe that kept him seated.

"Close yer eyes. Jus fer a second. It's okay."

David did as the old man said. Once his eyes were shut and he could only see darkness, Joseph's hand circled David's thin arm and squeezed, not tightly but with enough pressure for David to jolt back and open his eyes. "It's alright, son. I promise."

David closed his eyes again. After several seconds of staring into the complete darkness, he could see a faint light; it slowly stretched itself all around him. He could feel it.

Within his mind, he could hear Isaac. His brother's voice was loud, as if he was standing in the room beside David. The light grew brighter and brighter, and he found himself closing his eyes even tighter, turning his head away from the light. But there was no escape. And then the light dulled and he found himself in his parent's back yard. Standing next to him was Isaac, just as he had looked a month earlier. There was a smile on his brother's face, and David smiled in return.

In this dream-vision, David turned and looked back to the house and saw his parents standing on the small porch—they waved at the two boys and David waved back. He knew Isaac was doing the same. His parents were both smiling, laughing at some comment one of them had made. When David turned back to Isaac, the boy was gone and he found a grown man standing beside him. He knew this stranger was Isaac, a future version that his brother would never become. And David watched as this grown Isaac walked slowly away from him, moving toward the house, where their parents had been only seconds earlier. But their parents were gone now, and in their place was a woman, beautiful and tall, with brown hair that swirled in the breeze. And beside her was a young boy, maybe four years old. David watched as this future Isaac climbed the porch steps and then picked the boy up and held him high in the air. David could hear the boy's laughter, loud and filling the entire yard of David's imagination.

Just before the vision disappeared and David was left within the darkness of his closed eyes again, his brother turned to David and smiled and lifted his hand in a wave of greeting or thanks, or maybe it was just one of love. And then the three of them, along with the house and yard, were gone.

When David opened his eyes, he found that the old man no longer held his arm. Joseph was standing beside him now, a look of sadness clouding his face, making the deep lines around his nose and lips more pronounced.

"You did that." David spoke quietly.

"I'm sorry," Joseph said softly.

"He can't come back, though."

The old man shook his head. "What's done can't be undone."

"Then why'd you show me that?"

"He can't be made right, but I can show yeh how to keep others from feelin that same pain you felt, an they might grow up to have a life like yer brother won't."

"How?" David wiped tears away from his face.

"Here," Joseph said softly. He placed a small fabric doll on the table in front of the boy.

It was of a crude shape, andlooked homemade. Its skin was white and yellow, and it was dirty in places along the head and arms. There was no hair on the doll, no shirt. The pants were made of a thin black cloth that looked ragged and stretched. Old and worn. David was afraid to touch it, afraid of what power the small artifact might hold. It was the mystery object he'd seen the day before in the old man's hands.

David looked back to Joseph and then to the doll. His chest felt heavy. He looked down at the floor, next to the chair, and saw the box—he'd nearly forgotten about it. It was made of wood, slightly larger than the crate David's mother used for picking apples in the spring and autumn months. The box was full, nearly to the brim, with dolls; some had different shades of skin and they wore various colored pants, though each was a replication in size and quality of the one on the table.

"What is it?" David asked, looking up at the old man.

"It's us," Joseph said. "Any of us. All of us, maybe."

The boy searched for words, though there was nothing to say.

The old man smiled.

Joseph continued: "Each of these dolls is someone out there in the world. Ain't no tellin who, though. An as long as I can remember, I been wakin up to a full box. The dolls I fix, they're taken away. Can't tell yeh by who. Don't never see them again. All's I know is that it's my job to mend each doll. Though I can't say who it is gave me the job."

"You fix the dolls?" David asked as he studied the one resting on the table.

Joseph nodded. "I like to think I fix people."

"How?"

"I'll show yeh." The old man scratched at his face, brushing away dust or a tear, maybe. "Take up that doll there." The old man motioned to the table.

Sweat had started again on David's forehead and neck, though his hands remained dry; he was surprised by how steady and calm they were as he reached out and lifted the doll from the table. He held it at a distance in front of him, afraid it might come to life.

"Good," Joseph said quietly. "There's some loose stitchin on that doll. Somewhere. I can't tell yeh where it is. It changes fer each. Might be big or might be so small yeh have to look at it for minutes, movin yer hands over the skin and surface like yer readin its palm-future." He smiled. "Guess, in a way, you are, decidin its future."

David turned the doll over in his hands; he brought it close to his eyes and he smelled the fabric, musty and old, and sweet, like the petals of a flower he'd once smelled.

"Find it?" the old man asked.

Just as David was about to say no, he moved his finger over a spot in the fabric that was torn and frayed. It was small, almost unnoticeable, though the longer he looked at the opening, the larger it seemed to grow until it was the only thing that David could see when he looked down at the doll.

"Now yer gonna mend it."

"I don't know how," David answered.

"Yes, yeh do."

David could feel the old man's breath, hot on his neck. Then the boy's body became cool and peaceful.

"Take up that needle an thread there. I already set the thread through for yeh." David did as he was instructed. "Now, pull the thread til it's near the length a yer arm. When yeh done that, bite through it with yer teeth an tie a knot at the end, nice an small." David did this, too. "Good," Joseph said, as if he could see clearly the boy's actions through the fog of his cataracts.

"Find the tear an poke the needle through."

David did so but almost dropped the doll on the floor when he saw a small trickle of red liquid come from the new wound on the doll.

"Don't worry bout the blood. It's all part of what needs be done," the old man whispered.

Over the next five minutes or so, Joseph spoke to David in a calm voice, telling the boy the steps to stitching the seams of the torn doll. As Joseph spoke, his hand moved in front of him, weaving the air with his thin fingers, old with time, yet steady and dry in the humid shack. It was as if he was sewing an invisible doll, moving the needle and thread along with David, stitching and moving, letting his hand flow gently as he worked. Orchestrating the repair from a distance.

After David finished, Joseph brought his hand down to the boy's shoulder and let it stay there. The old man was out of breath, sweating. "Yeh did fine, son."

"How do you know?" David asked, though he did not move his eyes from off the doll that he now held tightly in his hands.

"I do is all." Joseph patted the boy's shoulder.

"How many of these do you fix each day?" David turned and looked at the old man.

"Lots," Joseph said quietly. "Never enough, though." There was no expression to his face, but David thought he saw several tears running down the old man's cheek. "Everbody's got some stitch come loose that needs mendin."

"And you fix them all?"

"Fast as I can."

David looked down at the box beside the chair. There were too many dolls in there to count.

"What if you run out?"

"Ain't never gonna happen. Each day I wake, that box there's full as the day previous. Don't know how it is, but it is. I learned that it's best not to ask questions to things you ain't rightfully true to know. Those answers might not be what yeh want to hear. That's jus somethin that yeh learn as yeh get older. Some day yeh'll come to understand."

David turned his attention back to the doll. The stitching was jagged and raw, though he could no longer see the hole that had once been there. The frayed material was gone and in its place was something genuine and, somehow, new.

"Does it really work?" David asked. He set the doll on the table in front of him and rubbed his thumbs over his fingers. "Does it actually fix someone?"

Joseph was silent for several seconds, and David turned to make sure the old man was still there. He was. After a while, the old man nodded slightly. Then he turned to David. "Don't reckon it really matters. That's how I always figured it. A big *What if*, I know. But that's how the most important things in the world are. *What ifs*, not *What if nots*."

The old man took several steps out into the room and then circled back to where David sat at the table. Then he eased himself slowly down so that he sat on the floor beside the box of dolls. "Things yeh'll learn over time. Here." He handed up several dolls from out the box. "These're yer wards now. Fix em. Help em."

David took the dolls and studied the blank faces, the tan material of the skin. "I can't."

Joseph smiled. "Yeh can, son. Always could. It's what yer meant for. Same as me." The old man was quiet for a minute. He shook his head and let a silent laugh escape his throat. "Get on outa here."

The boy studied the old man, who seemed to look out past the walls of the shack, out into the woodlands to where the waters ran cool and the shade kept the bright sun from your eyes. It was as if Joseph no longer knew David was there in the room with him.

After a minute or so, David stood and walked to the door, his arms full with the dolls he'd been handed.

As the boy was about to walk out of the shack, Joseph called to him. David turned.

"Might be a broken bone needs mendin. That's easy. But it might be a heart gone wrong from some lost love or a mind caught up in ugly thoughts or memories that can't rid its self of. Those last kinds are tricky. They need extra special care. Remember that."

David nodded to the old man and then he walked out into the woods, hearing the birds and small scurrying animals around him.

At his house, David set the dolls on Isaac's bed, and then he went to the downstairs closet. There, tucked deep in the shadow corners of the space, hidden behind old records his father once played and jackets that were changed colors with years of dust, David brought out his mother's sewing basket.

Back in the bedroom, David set about selecting the right needle, one similar in size to the one he'd used in the shack. He licked the end of the thread, as he'd seen his mother do, and then he threaded it through the needle's eye. He tied a small knot and then measured the thread to length, just as the old man taught him.

David lifted the first doll slowly and studied its blank features. He wondered who this person could be. What was his name? Or hers? Did she deserve to be saved, given another chance? But who was he to decide such things? he thought. And, with that, he took the thread and needle and poked it through the doll's flesh. He hesitated for a short moment, wondering if this person could feel the same prick, like a voodoo doll, but that was unimportant. And, so, he set to work, stitching the broken and scarred pieces together so that the frayed material joined.

Maybe one day he would find his parents' dolls, or his own, and stitch its parts together, and fix it, fix their hurt. And his own. There was no telling if any of this meant anything, if it was real or just some lie. But none of that seemed to matter as he tied a knot and cut the extra thread away. He looked at the doll, complete now in his hands.

He set the first doll down and then picked up the next one and studied its features; they were the same as the other, though there was a strange difference between the two. *This could be a child grown sick*, he thought, *A girl standing on the edge of a building. An old man in a hospital wanting to see his family once more.* There were so many possibilities, and he dared not think them all. He continued to look at the strange doll in his hands. Some day he might meet this person; it might be a friend, a lover. Some person who would wake tomorrow healed of pain, thankful to a boy they might never know.

Maybe the doll was everyone.

He smiled at this thought, though there were tears clouding his vision and streaming down his cheeks. He turned the doll over in his hands, searching for the broken seam. When he found it, he sunk the needle in and began to draw the thread through. On his fingertips he could feel the blood come from the doll and stain his skin. He could not see with his eyes full of tears, but he no longer needed sight. His fingers already knew the pattern by feel.

South of Salvation

Scene 1

The play will be comprised of four scenes. The first two scenes will be separated spatially on the STAGE (the first scene will be contained to STAGE RIGHT and the second scene will stay to STAGE LEFT). The LIGHTS will only come up according to the scene. This will allow for easy transition with set dressings. The third scene will take place on just a small portion of STAGE LEFT. The fourth scene, however, will play out on the entire STAGE and will require some set changing.

When the LIGHTS come up for Scene 1, we are only shown half of the STAGE. The setting here is a small corner-shop deli restaurant. We see a table with some cups and plates with food on them (sandwich rolls and some potato chips) and two chairs. A body occupies each chair. In the chair to STAGE RIGHT sits JAMES (a man in his early to mid-thirties: clean cut, dressed in jeans, sneakers, and a light jacket). JAMES should seem hesitant throughout the play, especially in this scene and the fourth. Sitting in the chair to STAGE LEFT is a large man dressed in a black suit, PORTER (we should be almost disgusted by this man—the way he eats, talks, his mannerisms, etc.). The chairs should be angled so that we can see in full all the action around the table. Next to PORTER, sitting on the ground, is a sleek black briefcase that the audience should not notice immediately. The play will begin in media res within their conversation.

PORTER
(smiling and leaning back in his chair)
You look a little confused, Mr. Richards.

JAMES
James.

PORTER
Alright, then. James. You are confused, though, I imagine. Yes?

JAMES
(nodding)
A little.

PORTER
I can understand that.

PORTER takes a big bite from the sandwich roll and then eats some of the potato chips without having swallowed the sandwich. He chomps away wholeheartedly at the food, brushing the crumbs from his suit, and then washes the partially eaten food down with the drink.

JAMES
I guess I just don't really understand what you want from me.

PORTER
(swallowing and patting his stomach)
You're right. It's pointless for me to sit here and sidestep around a cart of bullshit with you. So, I'll be straight with you.

JAMES
Okay.

PORTER
Okay. Here it is, then. Straight at you: one, two, three. You know what this is, I imagine.

PORTER reaches into his coat pocket and fishes around in there for something, which he eventually finds, and sets it down on the table. This action should correspond with a clear "TICK" sound.

PORTER
Yes?

JAMES says nothing, but looks down in silent shock.

PORTER
It's a bullet, James. Nothing special.
BEAT
But, I need you to take this here, and I need you to bury it in his head.

JAMES reaches out and grabs the bullet and looks around the room and then looks down at the bullet.

JAMES
(in a hushed yell)
What?! This is a joke, right? You're asking me to . . .

JAMES is interrupted by a waitress who comes over from the darkness of STAGE LEFT. JAMES clenches his fist tightly around the bullet and then looks up at her, panic spewing onto his face. PORTER smiles when he sees her.

WAITRESS
Can I get you guys anything more? Dessert? Anything?

PORTER
No thanks, honey. Why don't we just get the bill over here. My friend Jimmy here needs to get home. Starting to get a bit homesick. Aren't ya, Jimmy?

JAMES says nothing.

WAITRESS

Alrighty, then. Let me get that going for you guys . . .

(to JAMES)

. . . and get you home.

The WAITRESS smiles and EXITs STAGE LEFT. PORTER smiles, his eyes following her off.

PORTER

(jokingly)

She's a good lookin' gal now, ain't she, Jimmy?

JAMES is still silent. He looks back down at the bullet.

PORTER

You were saying?

JAMES

(in the same hushed yell)

What the hell am I supposed to do with this? I can't. You want me to kill someone? Really?

BEAT

(confused)

Are you a cop or something? Is this some kind of bust or something? Or a hidden camera thing? Because I haven't done anything wrong.

PORTER

(laughing)

No, no, no. I'm pretty damn far from a cop, actually. And there aren't any cameras, James. Go ahead and look around for yourself if you want.

JAMES

Seriously, man, if this is a joke then it's over. Look, Mr. Porter, you've had your fun, but I've gotta go. Really. I've already wasted enough time here.

JAMES gets up to leave.

PORTER
(angrily, changing his entire light-hearted nature from before)
Sit down, James!

PORTER grabs JAMES's wrist. JAMES looks down at the man and sits down slowly but doesn't look at PORTER.

PORTER
(soothingly)
This isn't a joke, James. It's an offer. Simply an offer. Nothing more. I need someone killed and I'm offering you the chance to do it. That's all.

JAMES
Who? Who is it you want me to . . .

PORTER
(losing patience)
Jesus Christ, James. Are you deaf? My god! The man I've been telling you about for the last hour. It's simple business: he screws with us—and even you agreed that what he did was pretty damn well bad—and he's gonna get it back in return. Retaliation's a bitch. Remember that, Jimmy. If there's one thing that I can impart to you today, it's that there are always consequences, James. Always.

JAMES
This doesn't make any sense.

JAMES finally looks up at PORTER. JAMES's eyes are filled with a sheepish confusion.

PORTER
The most important choices in life never do.

There is a moment of silence between them.

JAMES
(with an uncomfortable laugh, then timidly angry)
I've never even held a gun before. Did you know that? I would think that since you picked me you would have an idea that I'm a pretty bad choice.

PORTER
So, you've never shot a gun. So what? It's not that complicated. Watch enough TV and it's pretty much like it is there: point it, pull the trigger, make sure the guy's not breathing, walk away. Done deal.

JAMES
(shaking his head)
I can't do it. I can't kill anyone. The fact that I'm still here listening to your insane bullshit is crazy enough, but that's it. I can't do it.

PORTER
Why can't you? Religion?

JAMES
Morals, Mr. Porter. Morals and ethics and . . . and it's just wrong. I can't.

The WAITRESS comes back over and leaves the check. The two men remain silent while she comes over.

WAITRESS
No rush, guys. Whenever. I'll go ahead and take these, though.

PORTER smiles and thanks her. The WAITRESS takes the two plates and EXITS STAGE LEFT.

PORTER

Morals, religion, it's all the same thing.

JAMES takes the bullet and tries to hand it back to PORTER.

JAMES

Whatever it is, I can't. Here. I'm sorry I can't help you.

PORTER doesn't take the bullet back. JAMES sets it down on the table again with another "TICK," though this time it is quieter.

PORTER

Alright, James. But here . . .

PORTER takes the bullet and tosses it to JAMES, who catches it and looks at it again.

PORTER

Why don't you hold onto it just a second longer. Just one. First, before you say anything else, before you do anything else, why don't you take a look at who it is I'm asking you to—I don't want to sound too much like a movie, but why the hell not, right?—but take a look at who I'm asking you to handle for me.

PORTER reaches down, takes up the briefcase, and sets it on the table in front of him. He undoes the latches, which are loud, and then lifts the lid of the case. From inside, PORTER takes out a manila envelope and slides it over across the table to JAMES.

JAMES picks up the envelope, undoes the string sealing the envelope, and takes out the contents, which is just one photograph. JAMES's hands are shaking as he looks at the picture.

PORTER

(smiling)

He's changed a bit, I imagine.

PORTER closes the case and replaces it on the floor next to his feet.

JAMES
I don't know who this is.
(looking at PORTER)
Who is he?

PORTER
Take a closer look, yeah? I think you know.

JAMES looks back at the photo and stares intently at it for a few seconds before he looks up at PORTER in shocked recognition, letting the photo drop to the table in front of him.

JAMES
What . . .?

PORTER
I understand, James. I do. Just relax for a second. Take a breath. . . . Here, take a drink.

PORTER pushes JAMES's drink over to JAMES.

PORTER
And now focus on me . . . James.

JAMES looks around in complete confusion, looking to his left and right.

PORTER
James . . .

JAMES
I . . .
BEAT
(suddenly angry)
Why me? Huh? Why come to me with this?

PORTER
(smiling)
Why you?
BEAT
That's a legitimate question, I guess.

JAMES
(angrily)
Then give me a legitimate goddamn answer.
(shaking the photo at PORTER)
Why do you come to me? With this?! It makes no sense! Come to me and say go kill this guy and then show me who it is! Me! Nothing me!
BEAT
(becoming angry)
You come to me, out of nowhere, call me on the phone, say you can help my daughter, look me in the eyes here, and tell me I have to kill someone, and not just anyone, but . . . him.

PORTER
(calmly, almost amused)
I thought seeing who it is might have changed your mind a bit. Might settle any doubts you might have.

There is a long silence.

PORTER
Look, James. I know all about you. I know about when you grew up, where, I know all about your family. . . . My god, James, I probably know more about you than your wife does. I know everything there is to know about you. And, that means I also know all about your daughter.

JAMES looks up angrily at PORTER.

PORTER

Relax, James. That's how I got you here, is her. Isn't it? You just admitted that.

BEAT

Without her, you'd never be sitting here considering my proposition. Right?

PORTER bends over, undoes the briefcase, reaches inside, pulls a slip of paper from the case, and locks the latches, leaving it next to him. He looks down at the paper.

PORTER

Christine Richards, age seven. . . . Hmm. . . . There's a lot of big words here, James. Words I can't begin to try and say. And, if I know one thing, I know that big words from doctors usually means bad news for patients, yeah?

He pretends to read the sheet of paper intently and then looks up.

PORTER

Ah-ha, enlarged heart. I can read that one.

JAMES

(calmly, angrily)

How did you get that?

PORTER

I just told you, James. My god, you don't seem to hear well—you might need to stop in and check that out.

JAMES

How?

PORTER

I can get whatever I want, James. Information, papers, money, drugs . . .

BEAT

And, yes, James, I can get a heart.

JAMES

That's impossible. We've been on the list for four months.

PORTER

And in another four months, you won't have a daughter to worry about transplants or hospitals, or . . .

JAMES

Shut up! Shut the hell up! . . . Please . . .

PORTER

Unless . . .

PORTER scoots his chair closer to JAMES and theatrically "whispers" to JAMES.

PORTER

Unless I get her one. It won't be that hard for either of us. You simply shoot that man in the photo there, shoot him in the head, and I simply make a phone call and your daughter can keep being your daughter. You can buy her a bike for her birthday instead of flowers for her grave, yeah? Listen, James, I don't mean to sound heartless. That's not at all what I'm after.

JAMES wipes his eyes with his sleeves.

PORTER

(handing JAMES a handkerchief)

Here.

BEAT

You see, James, I try to look at myself as a philanthropist of sorts. You ask me why I chose you: I only want to help someone when I can. Now is one of those times that I can. And you are the person that I can help.

PORTER *slides back his chair abruptly, grabs his briefcase, and stands. JAMES watches him intently.*

PORTER
(matter-of-factly)
And, you're cheaper than anyone else I would hire. You can get close to him when someone else wouldn't be able. He won't even know.

JAMES *looks at the bullet, running his other hand through his hair.*

PORTER
The gun that goes with that is in your glove box, along with the address of where you'll find him. You have five days. If it isn't done by then, no hard feelings, that's fine, I'll find someone else. But you should probably think about praying to your God for your daughter's sake.
BEAT
See if he can't get her name up on that list they have. Huh?

JAMES
How do I know that you'll come through on your part?

PORTER
(smiling)
You don't, James. Faith alone. Faith alone.

PORTER *reaches into his pocket and pulls out a wad of money, takes a couple of bills, and sets them down on the table.*

PORTER
Lunch is on me, okay?

PORTER *turns and begins to walk to STAGE LEFT and then turns back.*

PORTER

What is it your Bible says, James? Sins of the father brought on the son, right?

PORTER turns, chuckling at himself, and EXITs.

JAMES watches PORTER leave and then sits silently at the table. He looks down at the bullet, puts it in his jacket pocket, and sits, lost in thought as the LIGHTS dim and then go out completely.

Scene 2

The LIGHTS open on STAGE LEFT. There is a couch and coffee table. On the table are books and magazines strewn here and there. We should have the feeling of a scattered messiness in the room. The couch is angled toward the audience. On the couch sits a woman, around the same age as JAMES. She is SARAH, JAMES's wife. She is dressed in sweatpants, her hair is pulled back in a tight ponytail, and she wears a loose-fitting sweatshirt. She shouldn't look like a slob, but rather like someone who is purely exhausted, physically and emotionally.

While she sits on the couch, SARAH frantically bounces her legs up and down. She rubs her face, pulls loose strands of hair from her eyes; she is always moving. She grabs her cell phone from next to her on the couch, dials a number, and puts it up to her ear. She waits a few seconds, then angrily tosses it next to her.

SARAH

Goddammit, James! Answer the phone!

She goes back to nervously bouncing her legs then reaches to the books and magazines and begins to organize them, but she cannot and reaches for the phone again, dials, and listens. While she is waiting for JAMES to answer, we hear the sound of a door open and shut at STAGE RIGHT. SARAH ends the call and puts it down. JAMES ENTERS from STAGE RIGHT; SARAH stands.

SARAH

Jesus Christ, James. Where the hell have you been? I've been trying to call you for hours now.

JAMES

I'm sorry.

JAMES begins to walk, passing behind the couch to EXIT STAGE LEFT.

SARAH

Sorry?!

JAMES

(angrily, turning around)

Yeah, Sarah. I'm sorry!

SARAH

Sorry?! Jesus. That's it, James? That's all you say? Goddammit. It's ten o'clock. I thought you were gonna go to the hospital with me. Christine kept wondering where you were; I told her you'd be coming any second. I tried calling you over and over and you never answered, and . . . Goddammit, James, I thought something happened, I thought you got in an accident, or something, and all I could think about when I listened to that goddamn doctor telling me the same shit that I've heard over and over and over and over again was you and wondering where you were and if you were okay and worried to death about you and then I come home and, for hours I sit here, calling you, afraid to get up and move in case you call and I miss it, and you come in and *sorry* is all you can say to me.

BEAT

Christ.

SARAH sits down heavily on the couch and buries her face in her hands. JAMES walks back to where she is, around the coffee table, and sits next to her. He puts his arms around her and she falls over, into his arms, crying heavily. JAMES rocks her back and forth, quietly whispering to her. Finally, she composes herself and pulls away and looks at him.

SARAH
(wiping her eyes, her expression a combination of concern and anger)
Where were you?

JAMES
I had a meeting. That's all. It wasn't anything bad. I promise, Sarah. Really. I didn't think it would last as long as it did. I'm sorry that I wasn't at the appointment. I'll talk to Chrissy in the morning. Okay?

SARAH
You had a meeting until ten o'clock, James? With who? That doesn't make any sense.

JAMES
It was with a client from work.

SARAH
(frustrated)
Please stop lying to me, James. Just stop.
BEAT
Just tell me the truth. Please.
BEAT
Are you seeing someone?

JAMES
What?! Sarah, come on.

SARAH
(sternly, but letting the emotions get the better of her)
James! Yes or no?!! Just tell me.

JAMES
No, Sarah! No! I can't believe you'd even think that. Honestly.

They sit in silence. JAMES rubs his hands over SARAH's legs, affectionately, but absent-mindedly. They both seem mentally removed: JAMES looks up at the ceiling, SARAH looks away to UPSTAGE. Finally, SARAH breaks the silence:

SARAH
(still looking away)
I'd understand.

JAMES
(bringing his attention to SARAH)
What?

SARAH
I'd understand if you were seeing someone. It wouldn't hurt me. I mean it would, but I'd understand it.

JAMES
Jesus, Sarah. I'm not seeing anyone else. I'm not. I promise you.
(soothingly and seriously)
Look at me, please . . .

JAMES gently holds SARAH's face and directs her attention and gaze to him. He brings his face up close to hers.

JAMES
There's no one else. I promise, sweetheart. Please believe me. I love you so much. Don't you understand that?

SARAH
I do. I do. And I love you, James. So much.
BEAT
But I just don't know how I can take it anymore. And I don't know how you can either. Any of this. I mean, I don't know what to do.
BEAT

At what point do we quit, James? What point do we give up what we're doing? Or what we're trying to do? I know things aren't the same between us since this all began with her. I know it. And I'm sorry, but I can't do it anymore. I can't pretend. I can't try.
(her voice begins to break; she is having a minor anxiety attack. Her hands begin to shake slightly)

I can't take it much longer, and I know you can't either.
BEAT

I don't know what to do, James. I'm sorry, James. I am. I'm so sorry. But I don't know what to do. I don't know. But I love you, James. As much now as I ever have. I know that. I just hope that someday this can all be over and we can be happy again.
BEAT

Do you think we can?

JAMES doesn't know what to say. He nods slightly.

SARAH

Do you?

JAMES

I do. I really do. I'm trying, too. And I know you are. And I'm so proud of you. You're such a great mother. Do you know that?

SARAH shakes her head. JAMES leans over and kisses her cheek. They separate and JAMES continues to rub her leg. They sit quietly, neither looking at the other. Finally,

JAMES

How did it go at the hospital?
BEAT

What did the doctor say?

SARAH

The same as always. Every day it's the same.

JAMES

If it's the same, then that doesn't mean it's getting any worse, though. Right?

SARAH

I don't know. I don't know.

JAMES

Did you ask about the list again?

SARAH

(shaking her head)

He said there's no chance of her getting moved up for at least six months, maybe more.

(she begins to cry)

But he said he doesn't even know if her heart can last that long.

(she begins openly weeping now)

He said he doesn't know. Oh God, James. Our baby! Our baby! What are we supposed to do? I can't. I can't.

SARAH is in hysterics now. JAMES holds her tightly and she sobs into his shirt. He whispers soothing "Shhhs" to her as he gently rubs her back. Eventually, she begins to calm down and they are quiet, JAMES holding her tightly. Over her head, JAMES looks around at the room, as if judging it for its worth.

There is a long silence between them. Then, seemingly out of nowhere:

JAMES

How far would you go to make something right?

SARAH breaks away from JAMES's hold and dries her eyes with her sleeves. She looks at him.

SARAH

What?

JAMES

I don't know. I've just been thinking, I guess.

BEAT

I've been thinking all day about it. But, I guess I'm just trying to figure something out, you know.

BEAT

I don't know, Sarah. Do you think it's alright to do something bad if it's for a good reason?

SARAH

I don't know. Like what?

JAMES

You know, like the greater good thing: do one thing wrong so that something good can come from it. Does that make sense?

SARAH

Yeah. A little.

JAMES

But what do you think, though?

SARAH

I don't know. Like what kind of bad thing?

JAMES

I don't know. I'm just thinking out loud.

SARAH

(thoughtfully)

I don't know. It depends, I guess.

JAMES

Depends on what?

SARAH

On how important that one thing is.

BEAT

JAMES

What if it's *that* important?

BEAT

SARAH

Then you have to do what you can, I guess.

The two sit in thought. James stares at the floor, SARAH back to UPSTAGE. After a few seconds, she rubs his hands a little, then gets up and begins to walk off to STAGE LEFT. She stops and looks back at JAMES, still sitting on the couch: he hasn't moved.

SARAH

(tenderly, lovingly)

Are you coming to bed?

No response. JAMES is still lost in his own thoughts.

SARAH

(still tenderly and lovingly)

James?

JAMES finally hears her and looks up. He smiles sadly at her.

SARAH

(same)

Are you coming to bed?

JAMES

I'll be in in a second.

SARAH

Okay.

SARAH begins to walk off.

JAMES
Sarah . . .

She turns and looks at him.

JAMES
I love you.

SARAH
(with a sad smile)
I love you, too.
(hesitantly)
Come in soon. Okay?

SARAH EXITs STAGE LEFT. JAMES is left sitting by himself on the couch. He looks around the room, lost. Then he reaches into his pocket and fishes out the bullet and looks at it, examining it. He sighs heavily and then puts the bullet away in his pocket.

The LIGHTS go down slowly on JAMES, sitting by himself. Finally, the room goes completely dark.

Scene 3

The LIGHTS come up on STAGE LEFT. All we can see is a door (facing from STAGE RIGHT to STAGE LEFT). The LIGHTS only illuminate what is to the STAGE LEFT side of the door; STAGE RIGHT remains in complete darkness. The door is freestanding.

The STAGE remains like this for a little while before JAMES ENTERs from STAGE LEFT. He is dressed in jean pants and a large coat, one that looks maybe a bit too big for him. He approaches the door slowly. When he reaches it, he looks from side to side—we assume he is looking up and down the street. He is cautious. JAMES reaches into his left coat pocket and pulls out the gun, once again looking nervously from side to side. He looks at it and shakes his head a little, then puts it in his pocket and begins to walk off STAGE LEFT, but he stops, takes a deep breath, and turns around. He approaches the door quickly and knocks on the wood. The sound echoes through the STAGE. There is no answer, so he knocks again—this time harder and longer. We can hear the sound of shuffling, a cleared throat, movement coming from STAGE RIGHT, but it is still in darkness and we can only wait. JAMES puts his ear to the door, then backs away and knocks again. From STAGE RIGHT we can hear someone at the door, still hidden in the shadows. JAMES is about to knock one more time, but the door opens. Whoever it is that opens the door (STEPHEN) still remains in the dark of the shadows. JAMES takes a short step back.

STEPHEN
(just his voice)
Yeah? What do you want?
BEAT
Huh?

JAMES tries to speak but can't. STEPHEN shuts the door. From inside the house and through the door:

STEPHEN
I ain't buyin' whatever the hell you're selling, so get off my doorstep and get the hell out of here.

JAMES remains in front of the door, seemingly shocked. He reaches his hand into his pocket; we can tell he's holding the gun. He knocks on the door with his right hand; his left remains in his pocket. The door opens quickly, as if STEPHEN has been waiting by the door.

STEPHEN
Goddamn it, boy. Get the hell outta here. I swear, I'll call the cops if you don't get.

JAMES
(strongly, loudly)
Take a look. One look.

BEAT

STEPHEN
Yeah? At what?

BEAT

JAMES
At your son.

JAMES takes another breath, one that is shaky. There is a long silence while JAMES stands at the door.

STEPHEN
James? No . . .

BEAT

JAMES nods his head slowly.

STEPHEN
(in disbelief)
My God. How are you here?
BEAT
Jesus, James. I can't. . . . My God. Do you want to come in, or...? Jesus . . .

As JAMES walks into the house, the LIGHTS go down and then the door shuts in the darkness.

Scene 4

There should be just a short break between Scene 3 and Scene 4. When the LIGHTS do come up, we see the whole STAGE. At CENTER STAGE there is a wooden kitchen table with four chairs set around it—the table should be angled so that the audience can fully see the two at their respective seats at the table. JAMES sits in a chair that is further toward STAGE LEFT. He is alone, his coat still on. Though the audience will not notice it, JAMES's left hand is in his coat pocket—he will remain this way for a majority of the scene, unless otherwise noted.

JAMES looks around the small room (which consists of a couch and a wooden table with a television set on it, all of which are located behind and to the left of JAMES). After a little while, STEPHEN comes in, carrying two beers. STEPHEN is an older man, with gray and white hair, a bit pudgy but not fat, and he wears glasses (the kind that were popular in the late seventies and early eighties). He is dressed in jeans, a white shirt, and boots. STEPHEN sets the beers on the table and pulls out a bottle opener. He opens the two bottles and hands one of them to JAMES. JAMES takes the beer, drinks a sip, and sets the bottle down on the table in front of him. STEPHEN takes a seat at the chair that is further toward STAGE RIGHT. He settles himself, takes a drink, sets the bottle down, and then slides the bottle slowly from left to right in front of him, trying to keep himself busy, trying to break the awkward silence. STEPEHEN stops moving the bottle and looks up, his hand still holding the beer.

STEPHEN

Look, I can take that coat of yours. It's pretty hot in here.

JAMES

(short and direct)

It's alright.

STEPHEN

You sure? I can go turn the air conditioner up if you want.

JAMES
(short and direct)
It's okay. Really.

STEPHEN
Alright then.

STEPHEN takes another sip of the beer and sets the bottle down again. JAMES looks around the room. There is a long, awkward silence between the two. Finally, STEPHEN talks, bringing JAMES's attention back to the man across from him.

STEPHEN
(with an unsteady voice, almost hoarse-sounding)
How's your mom?

JAMES
(short, direct, and angry)
Dead.

STEPHEN
Oh . . . I'm sorry about that. I didn't know.

JAMES
(short and direct)
I know you didn't. If you did, you wouldn't have asked.

JAMES takes a sip of beer. His face is set and hard.

STEPHEN
She was a really good person, your mom. But you know that, I'm sure.

JAMES
(near angry)
Yeah. She was.

JAMES brings the bottle up to his face, looks through the dark glass, and begins to read the label to himself.

STEPHEN looks at JAMES quietly, almost sadly.

STEPHEN

So, you probably've hated me all your life. Yeah?

JAMES sets the bottle down and then looks at his father; there is a true sincerity in the old man's face.

JAMES

I never knew you enough to hate you.

STEPHEN

Well.

BEAT

You should know that it wasn't you or your mom. . . . Okay? It wasn't either of you did anything wrong.

JAMES

I appreciate that, but I gotta be honest and tell you that I don't really care about it right now. What's done is done as far as I'm concerned.

STEPHEN

Yeah, but, James . . .

JAMES

(cutting STEPHEN off)

I learned how not to be a father. I can thank you for that.

STEPHEN

Do you have a family? Jesus. The things that happen when you don't look for them.

JAMES
(dryly)
Or when you don't see what's in front of you.

JAMES lifts the bottle up to the light, examines it, then takes a drink.

STEPHEN scratches his head, brushes his hand through his hair, and looks at JAMES sadly.

STEPHEN
Look, James, I understand you're angry at me. I do. And you've got every reason to be. But why come here now just to be angry? Why find me just to make me feel bad? . . . I'm sorry for what I've done to you and your mom. I truly am, but I don't need any help understanding the problems and the consequences of my decisions.

JAMES nods his head slowly. He looks around the room again, then back to STEPHEN.

JAMES
(trying to be nice)
I have a wife and a daughter.

STEPHEN
(smiling)
My God, James. . . . How old?

JAMES
She'll be eight in May.

STEPHEN
(still smiling—even bigger now)
Eight. What's that put her, first grade?

JAMES
Third, actually.

STEPHEN
(nodding his head)
Third. Yeah. Damn, I remember third grade. Christ, that was a long time ago.

STEPHEN scratches his head.

STEPHEN
Mrs. Bosworth was my teacher, I think. Or, maybe that was fourth or fifth grade? Too long ago to remember.

STEPHEN places his hands on the table, then scratches his left hand with his right.

STEPHEN
Do you have any photos?

JAMES
No.

JAMES takes a drink of beer.

BEAT

STEPHEN
How are they, your daughter and wife?

JAMES's hand in his coat pocket moves slightly, almost unnoticeably. He sets the beer back down.

JAMES
Okay. Things are okay, I guess. But I think they'll be fine.

STEPHEN
(smiling)
Things have a way of working themselves out, you know?

JAMES

They do, I guess. Yeah.

BEAT

I hope so, at least.

STEPHEN looks down at his watch.

STEPHEN

I'll be right back. Gotta take a leak. But look, if you want anything to eat or anything, feel free. I think I got some crackers or something in the cupboard and some bread and meat in the fridge if you want.

STEPHEN slides the chair noisily back and stands and EXITs STAGE RIGHT.

JAMES stares at the bottle in front of him for several seconds, moving his right hand over the table, feeling its smoothness. After a while, he stands and begins to walk around the room. He walks over to the table with the television on it, swipes his finger across the screen, and looks at it—we can assume his finger is covered with dust—and then he wipes his finger on his pants. He rubs his feet over the floor and looks around at the floor. He turns back to the table with the TV and closes his eyes. His left hand comes out of his pocket finally and he brushes his fingers through his hair. He squats down and rubs his eyes; we can see that he is visibly breathing hard. Over toward STAGE RIGHT we hear the sound of a door shutting; JAMES stands and watches STEPHEN ENTER from STAGE RIGHT. The old man shuffles over to the table and sits as he had been. JAMES walks over to the table and sits, also. STEPHEN takes a drink and sets the beer down, moving it across the table's surface again.

STEPHEN

You want another?

JAMES

I'm okay.

STEPHEN
Alright.

There is a silence between them. STEPHEN takes a deep breath. JAMES takes another sip of the beer. Finally:

STEPHEN
Back in the war—I don't know if your mom told you this, but I was in Vietnam.

JAMES shakes his head no.

STEPHEN
Well, I was. That's where we met, actually. She was a nurse—you probably know that, though. Married her after only a month and a half of knowing her. But anyways, I'm sidetracking a bit, but when I was over there, in the jungle out there, we always tried to keep ourselves busy. An idle mind there and you might as well stick your own gun in your mouth and pull the damn trigger is what we always said. But, we'd play cards, all types of games, you know: Poker, Fish, Rummy. Sometimes we even made up our own. Anyway, we had this one guy, used to call him Black Jack. Son of a bitch could play cards, I'll tell you. That's how he got his name—one hell of a card player—plus that boy was black as midnight. A real dark guy, but a good guy, though. Really good. He was the kinda guy you want behind you in a place like that.

STEPHEN takes a drink of the beer and sets it back on the table. JAMES slowly, almost imperceptibly, moves his hand to his coat pocket.

STEPHEN
One night, though, we were stuck off in the jungle. Whole goddamn place is a jungle, mind you, but me and Jack are just sitting there, just the two of us up against this big stump of a thing. And he's got his cards out, shuffling them, trying to get me to play. And I can hear explosions off in the background—got to be a

normal thing—I still wake some nights hearing them—but after a while of sitting there, and listening to him talk about playing, I look at him and ask him, I say, 'Are you afraid to die?' Those days, it seemed a natural question to ask. Over there it surrounds you until it becomes part of you. I used to stop some days and think about it, but Jack, he just stopped shuffling and looked straight at me and he says, 'No. I ain't afraid to die.' And he goes back to shuffling them cards and then he looks back at me and says, 'I guess I'm more afraid of living than dying.' Says, 'We all die. Everyone dies. That's easy.' But then he stops shuffling the cards and looks at me and gets all serious—which for him was something new—and he says, 'To look back at the end and see that you didn't really live and try new things, test your limits, test God if He's there, that's a hell of a lot scarier to me. It's a lot harder to live than to die, Stevie,' he says. I didn't pay much attention to it, but then two mornings after I found him out there in the jungle. And there he was, shot some twenty times or more.

STEPHEN stops for a second and stares off into the distance. His eyes are watery and he wipes them with the back of his hands.

STEPHEN
(quiet, somber)

I can still see his face, James. Eyes shut, blood in his hair.

BEAT

And that's when I really started to think about what he'd said to me and I realized that a person's life is all his own, you know? Why pull someone into something they don't want? Or that you don't want for them?

BEAT

After I got back . . . life, all of it, seemed slow, boring. I tried to live the normal life and settle down, have a kid, raise a family. But on those long nights, with your mom sleeping next to me, I would think of Jack. And finally I realized I wasn't really living the life I wanted and I wasn't gonna be living it if I kept it all up like it was. So I left. . . . I figured the two of you would be better without me there anyways, better off without me lying to myself, telling myself

I was happy, or telling you I was . . . pretending for you. Pretending that I was content, you know? I mean, if I had, if I kept it up, I would have just been dragging the two of you down with me.

JAMES looks at his father. STEPHEN's eyes are wet; his lips quiver gently. JAMES takes his left hand out of his pocket and sets it on the table—both his hands are in front of him.

STEPHEN

I know you don't care. But for me—that was for me. I needed to say it. And I'm glad you heard it. Maybe you . . . I don't know if it means anything, but I am truly sorry, James. I can understand if you can't, though. But I'm sorry.

The two sit in complete silence, neither man wanting to look at the other. After a while, James brings his left hand up and brushes his hair back with it. JAMES smiles and then shakes his head from side to side.

JAMES

What can I say? What should I say? Huh? I forgot about you. You know why?

BEAT

Because I never remembered you. I've seen maybe five pictures of you ever. All in boxes, all on accident. I forgot about you.

STEPHEN

(quietly)

Then why did you come here?

JAMES's hand moves quietly and slowly to his pocket.

JAMES

I . . .

JAMES stands and begins to walk back into the room behind him, over to the television table and then he looks back to STEPHEN, who is sitting at the table, not looking at JAMES; STEPHEN's eyes remain fixed on the table before him, studying some unknown place.

JAMES

What happened to you? Where'd you go? I mean . . . You say you had to go out and live . . . what was that life you lived? What was it that you left us for? . . . Was it worth it?

STEPHEN

(finally looking up at JAMES)

I . . .

BEAT

I've seen the world, James. I can say that. Things come in grays you know. I could say it was worth it, and I can say it wasn't. But the thing that I'm proud of is that I did it. I've seen the good, and I've seen the bad. I've been part of both. I've had mistakes, some bigger than the normal man, I guess. Some people like me and others don't, and, to be honest, I really don't care all that much who thinks what. But, I've lived, James. I've learned, I've experienced. . . . And, to me, that's all I ever needed.

STEPHEN puts his elbows on the table in front of him and puts his head in his hands. He seems exhausted.

JAMES looks at STEPHEN and then down at his own feet. From his coat pocket he pulls out the gun, slowly, hesitantly. JAMES looks back at STEPHEN sitting there, his head in his hands. JAMES takes a deep breath and lets it out unsteadily.

STEPHEN brings his head up and looks at JAMES standing before him with the gun in his hand.

STEPHEN

They got to you, huh? They got you to do it?

JAMES

What'd you do? They told me some story about you, but I need to know from you, I need to hear it. What'd you do? What made them come to me for this?

STEPHEN
(gently)
I could tell you, but it wouldn't make much of a difference. Would it? I'm not gonna sit here and tell you I don't deserve it and I'm not gonna say I do.
BEAT
But now, my last hope for you, for me, after getting to see you again and talk to you for once, I hope you remember me the way you want. Remember me the way I am now. The way you are now. And if you hate me forever, go ahead and think that and remember me that way, and that's your choice and I respect it. But I want you to know that seeing you here today has meant more to me than I could have ever thought.

JAMES looks down at his hand and then back up to his father. His face looks lost, confused, devastated.

STEPHEN
(gently)
Let me just ask one thing, though . . . Will it be worth it? For you to do this?

JAMES stares blankly at STEPHEN. STEPHEN's face is set—there is no pleading there, no sadness or hope.

JAMES
(quietly, almost a whisper)
It will.

STEPHEN lets out a shallow sigh and then smiles weakly, sadly.

STEPHEN
Why don't you come behind and do it. It'll be easier on both of us.

JAMES stands still for a second, then slowly moves around the table, keeping his distance from the seated man. Finally, JAMES stands behind his father. JAMES wipes a tear from his eye and stands quietly, breathing heavily. STEPHEN continues to sit with his gaze directed at the table in front of him. STEPHEN lifts the bottle to his lips and drinks, then sets the bottle on the table and pushes it away from him. STEPHEN wipes the water from the bottle off the table, rubs his hands together, and finally folds them in front of him.

JAMES, with strained effort, raises the gun. We can see that his hand is shaking slightly. STEPHEN takes in a deep breath then lets out a muffled, shallow sigh. JAMES clicks off the safety and directs the barrel at the back of his father's head. His hand begins to shake even more, there are tears in his eyes. He holds it there for several seconds. The LIGHTS dim on the two figures on STAGE until we are left in complete dark and then, finally, we hear the shattering sound and see the bright, quick flash of the gunshot that erupts through the quiet. The STAGE remains in complete darkness and silence for a while.

END

The After

a novella

Morning Light

Eduard Meyer stared up at the shadow ceiling of the cave, afraid to move and awaken himself fully from the dream he had been having. It was a dream of the ocean. While he lay there, he thought he could still feel the cold water on his ankles and the sand beneath his bare feet, the sounds of gulls crying all around him. But those feelings were not real, merely imagined.

It wasn't until he looked over and saw the thin streak of sunlight on the ancient rock a short distance away that the phantom tingle of the dream-waves left his skin and Eduard knew he was no longer dreaming. He remembered the evening previous and how she had come from out the shadows of the woods, and he turned away from the opening of the cave to look farther within, to the spaces that the day's light could not reach.

Several steps from where he lay was the shape of the strange woman. She was huddled against the wall of the cave, a wool blanket spread over her sleeping form, and he watched her from this distance, his head resting heavily on the stone bed. Her body rose and fell gently beneath the blanket. Beyond where she slept was the old man, and though Eduard did not see him in the darkness, he could hear the strained rasp of his breath, and he knew that the old man was still sleeping, as well.

Eduard sat up slowly, his body aching from the the cave floor, and rubbed his eyes so that specks of stars appeared in the blackness. The faint trickle of water echoed deep within the cave, reminding him of the place he once called home. It seemed a separate lifetime ago, how, in the dark mornings, he would walk to the river and sit along its bank. There, he would watch the morning light color the world around him and warm his body. After a while sitting, he would get up and dust himself off and walk back to the farm, back to his wife and all that he knew. Those were moments of the past; Eduard had tried to forget those moments, to secret them away in his memory, but he could not.

He climbed to his feet and walked quietly over to where the woman slept. Standing within the cave, he needed to hunch his back and duck his head low. Over the four years he'd been there, Eduard had come to learn where the lower-hanging parts of the ceiling were, and he knew to avoid them. Beneath his hair, he figured he had a dozen or so scars from striking his head against the rock within the darkness.

Beside where she lay was the makeshift fire pit that the old man constructed even before Eduard found his way to the cave. The pit was a circle of stones three feet in diameter, and in the middle were the charred remains of wood—bark and branches cut in half—from the past several weeks. Ash coated the ground within the stone circle, having turned the floor there a permanent black, and the smell of charred wood, of smoke and dust, seemed to fill the entire cave. Eduard could feel the gentle movement of cool air from within the cave's belly. The air that ushered the smoke from the fire to the cave's entrance and stained the ceiling and walls a charcoal gray as it journeyed outside. Eduard often wondered what stories the smoke had etched into the cave's walls: Would it one day give proof that he existed in that place, if even for a short while? or would the smoke simply cover up all trace of his life there?

Now, when he looked down at the center of the fire pit, Eduard could see—just beneath some of the larger branches that had not yet burned completely—several embers still glowing from the night before. He wondered if he should use them to start the fire anew, but, instead, he knelt down so as to see the woman more clearly in the darkness. It had been years since he'd been this close to a woman. He wanted to touch her arm, to feel her, to lay his hand upon her chest and feel her heart beating within. To make sure that she was real and not some strange illusion his loneliness had conjured. And so, he reached out toward her, though he did not continue. Instead, Eduard held his hand above her body for several seconds, willing himself to go on, but he was unable to. "How did you come to be here?" he whispered. He was silent for several seconds, as if waiting for her to wake and answer.

"How did any of us?"

He stood and turned away from her and walked toward the sunlight at the cave's entrance, the whole while feeling his hand shake from some desire he could not fully understand.

Runaway

There were several dozen of them, forty, maybe fifty at most, each alike in both face and clothing. They looked to be strange clones of one another in their gray uniforms, black boots, their helmets with the swastika and eagle hidden by mud and other debris the men had coated on the headgear. The mud and colors camouflaged them, hid them in their surroundings. In the evenings, they each could walk several hours, through different terrain, both flatland and forest, and not realize that the man walking to their left or right was even there, save for the sound of rocks crunching beneath his boots.

They were young men, their ages ranging from late teens—like Hans Kreuger, who kept pace beside Eduard but never spoke more than a word or two, and only in answer to a direct question—to mid-twenties, like Eduard himself.

Over the past several months, they had made their way from Berlin to the French border by way of rail and vehicle convoy. It wasn't until they arrived at Metz that Eduard and the men he was with broke off from the others. His group was ordered to search the small villages in the northeast of France—those places not listed on any map—and capture them in the name of the Reich.

Many of these places lay empty of humans. Birds flapped their paper wings loudly as they flew from out the upper windows of structures that had been built centuries earlier. The men often came across a wolf or some other creature roaming the cobbled streets of one of these villages, and the men would take aim and shoot the animal down. They ate the meat on those nights, passing the steaming pieces around. In the mornings, when they set out to the next village, the men left behind the skin and fur of the animal as if in warning to others who might come.

Occasionally, they would come across a village still occupied by men and women. The soldiers would spread out and enter at different places around the perimeter, making their way quickly toward the center. The majority of the soldiers would scream directions in German and what little French they knew to the panicked people, who ran this way and that. The rapid blast of fire from different guns would sound and echo throughout the regions where these villages were located, sounding as if there were three times as many soldiers as there really were. Several times, one of the villagers would take up a gun, usually an ancient pistol or hunting rifle, and take shots at the gray-clothed invaders, though this resistance never lasted long, as one or more German soldier would be there to shoot down the rebel.

The soldiers would gather the remaining villagers together in the center of the village and line them up along a wall. Twenty or so soldiers would point their *Maschinepistoles* at the various women and children and elderly men standing there. An edict establishing German control of the village would be recited by the captain, first in German and then translated to the villagers in French by one of the lieutenants. And then, an hour later, the soldiers would exit the village, leaving behind them villagers crying in fear and worry of what was next to come.

The German soldiers made their way deep into France in this manner. They cut paths through woodland areas no man's foot had ever stepped; each soldier carried his *Maschinepistole* pointed downward in front of him, and on each man's hip was a Walther pistol. Every few steps, Eduard's eyes would move quickly back and forth, looking for movement, color, something that seemed out of place in the darkness of his surroundings. While he did this, Eduard knew that those men around him were doing the same, and this gave him a strange comfort, some reassurance that he was not alone in this world after all.

They would stop at strange intervals on their journey. Those men in charge, the captain and two lieutenants, would radio in coordinates and receive updates from Berlin on where they were headed next. Whispers passed amongst the men during the nights hinting that Paris was their eventual destination, that they would meet up with the rest of the *Wehrmacht* before they reached the outlying parts of the city and, together, take control for the *Führer*.

When they did stop, Eduard, along with the others, would sit on the ground, or on a stump or rock if they were lucky; many of them would try to listen in to what was being said on the radio and in the private conversations between the captain and lieutenants. Depending on the time of day or evening, several of the men would wander off in search of food, either boar or deer, though they often only returned with berries and other vegetation they'd found. On the occasion they did find meat; those who'd gone off on the hunt would bring the animal back, dragging it through the dirt by a rope that all three or four men tugged at. The men who stayed behind to rest were then called on to start a fire and slice up the animal's body so as to more easily cook the meat, either in pans or on skewers made of branches.

On nights when they sat around the fire laughing at one another and the stories they told of times from before the war, Eduard would look at the scattered men and smile, knowing that, if for only this moment in time, he was just another soldier within the collective group. That he was ultimately unimportant and nameless.

What training he had was short and basic. In Berlin, he was given a uniform and shown how to shoot the several guns he would be required to carry.

Ultimately, he knew nothing of what to expect. The small moments of gunfire and battle he had been part of in the villages were quick, often lasting only thirty seconds or so before the man or woman—as it so often was—was shot down. And though he knew that death surrounded him in this world and followed him and the others wherever they journeyed, Eduard had not yet witnessed the real extent of what war looked like.

By the sun's height, Eduard guessed it was sometime around ten in the morning when they came to the stop. It was a small clearing covered in ferns that stretched off into the forest in every direction he looked.

Several of the men stood around while others sat on the ground, some using their helmets as seats. The few men who still had cigarettes left in their packs stood or sat smoking. Eduard thought about sitting too, as his legs were tired and cramped from walking. They hadn't come upon a village in several days but had, instead, simply walked through the thickening forests. Eduard took the moment to go and relieve himself a distance away; he wandered off beyond the group and pulled his pants to his ankles and was about to squat down when he heard the gunfire begin.

At first, Eduard thought it was merely some of the men taking shots at a boar or deer, but then the few stray shots increased in number and frequency. Within seconds, Eduard could only hear the whining shots and exploding eruptions of bullets being fired and tearing into trees and rocks and bodies, and he dropped to his hands and knees. Beneath the sound of gunfire, Eduard could faintly hear the screams of men, both in injury and confusion, and the shouts of orders, though he could not make out a single word. He pulled his pants up quickly to his waist and buckled his belt, though this took several seconds from the heavy shaking of his hands.

Eduard grabbed tightly to his *Maschinepistole,* which he had set down on the ground beside him only a minute or two before. A short distance away from him was a close gathering of beech trees, and he scrambled over the ground to them as quickly as he could move, keeping his head low to the earth, not paying any attention to the rocks and twigs and needles that cut into his hands.

When he reached the trees, he stood. His hands were cramped from holding onto the gun so tightly, and his temples throbbed along with his legs. His stomach felt tight, and he turned and vomited on the ground beside him. Tears were in his eyes, though he did not realize this. Instead, his attention was only on the sound of gunfire and screams coming from the clearing a short distance away.

As he wiped his mouth with the sleeve of his coat, he heard the first blast. Even from the distance away, he felt the explosion and knew that a grenade had been thrown. Without realizing what he was doing, Eduard dropped his gun and threw his arms around the beech tree in front of him, hugging the protecting giant as tightly as he could while the sound of grenade explosions and gunfire and screams circled around him in a chaos he could not begin to comprehend.

He remained like this for a long time, digging his face into the bark of the tree and willing himself not to let his legs go out from under him. When the frequency of gunshots slowed, he finally loosened his grip on the tree and stepped away; he turned so his back was to the clearing.

Without understanding why, Eduard began to walk forward, away from the men he had come to know as family. Away from whatever pain had come to pass there. He moved slowly, having no idea where he was headed, accepting whatever fate might find him in those next moments.

It seemed to Eduard that with each step he took away from the clearing, the sounds of the gunfire quieted, until finally, after fifteen minutes or so of walking without direction, the sounds of violence simply disappeared and he was left alone to listen to the wind moving through the trees around him and the birds calling his name from high up on branches, calling in either celebration or requiem.

He kept walking, and then he saw it. A small opening in the side of a hill. An opening no more than three feet in width, four feet in height.

Eduard walked slowly to the opening and ducked his head low and entered the cave.

The Old Man

There was no way of telling how deep the cave cut into the side of the hill.

Eduard stood quietly for a while, looking around him at the stone walls, but he could see nothing yet. He rubbed at his face with the palms of his hands, feeling the stubble on his chin and on his cheeks. After several seconds, he was able to make out faint outlines within the darkness. Somewhere deep within the cavern was the sound of water and, for the first time since the gunfire and explosions began, Eduard felt thirsty. He wondered how far off the water might be, and he began to walk toward the sound of it. With each step he took, the world behind him disappeared a little more, until he was so far in that he could not see the suncracked opening he had walked through only moments earlier.

After twenty steps more, Eduard was stopped by a sharp scraping sound of something moving across the rock floor. Eduard's breath caught, and his right hand moved directly to his hip, where he pulled the pistol from its hold. Though he could not see more than several inches before him, Eduard leveled the pistol, aiming it at the darkness. He wondered what strange beasts might exist in this place. If not for the fear he felt in that moment, he might have sat on the cold rock floor and cried in surrender, accepting whatever might come.

He heard the scraping sound again.

"Who's there?" he asked. His voice remained calm, despite the pounding in his chest.

Only silence and the far-off sound of the water answered. No scurry of rodent, no flap of wing, no child's cry or demon's voice. He asked again, and again he was answered with silence.

With the pistol still leveled in front of him, Eduard began to move in the direction he had just come. He dared not turn his back to the cave's heart, and so his progress was slow. If he had turned to look, Eduard would have seen the figure watching him from the entrance of the cave.

It wasn't until Eduard was only three or four steps away that the figure reached out a hand and placed it on Eduard's forearm.

When he felt the stranger take hold of him, Eduard turned and fired the pistol wildly around him. But the figure did not let go of Eduard's arm.

"*Nej. Nej, nej, nej,* Shh. Shhhh," the figure yelled in a strained and scratched voice.

When Eduard realized the pistol would fire no more, he turned away quickly and began running into the dark cave, but he tripped and fell over one of the many small boulders there. He tried to brace himself for the fall, but even with his hands stretched before him, the side of his head crashed heavily onto the stone floor. What little light he could see in the cave was replaced with an impenetrable blackness.

Eduard opened his eyes to flames dancing in front of him. Sweat was beading and dripping down his face from the heat, and his whole body felt warm and heavy. He tried to lift his head, but a hand gently came down on the side of his face and directed him back to the ground. "*Inte* än," a voice said. It was the same voice he'd heard earlier, calm and quiet; and though he could not understand the language, he allowed his head to remain there. After several seconds of watching the flames, Eduard closed his eyes once again and drifted off to sleep.

The fire was still burning when Eduard woke again. He was unsure of how much time had passed, and he slowly lifted his head to sit up. In the firelight, he could see the cave clearly. The dark shadow of his body moved along the walls in the flickering light. His head throbbed still, and when he reached up with his hand to touch his face, he felt the crust of dried blood.

Tears formed in his eyes and began to roll down his nose and lips and chin, and he wiped them away with his sleeve. It wasn't until he moved his hand away from his face that he saw the other man sitting across the fire from him.

He was an old man, nearly bald with the exception of several strands of white hair that lay flat on the top of his head. He wore loose fitting rags that looked at first to be a blanket draped over his shoulders and spilled onto his lap. In the darkness of the cave, with only the inconstant light of the fire between them, Eduard studied the old man. The man had squinted eyes that looked at first to be closed, and a vacant smile seemed constantly spread across his face.

Eduard raised his right hand in greeting to the old man, who only nodded in return, though, in that moment, this gesture was enough for Eduard.

After a day, the old man helped Eduard up, and they walked together, the old man guiding the younger around the darkness of the cave. As they walked, the old man held tightly to Eduard's arm, and Eduard felt a strange comfort in feeling the touch of another person again.

Few words were spoken between them, and what words were uttered could not be understood by the other. Their language quickly became gestures in the half-light: points of fingers, nods or shaken heads, gentle guiding pats on the shoulder.

During those first few days, the old man fed him a warm soup made from water and roots and leaves; several times, the old man added berries he'd collected, which turned the liquid a hazy purple.

After the fourth day of being within the cave, Eduard ventured outside for the first time. While the old man frequently came and went, Eduard was still too afraid of what he might find beyond the darkness of that place.

The sun blinded him, and he spent several minutes covering his face with his hands until his pupils constricted enough for him to see. Outside, as in the cave, Eduard was surprised at the quiet of the world around him. He wandered into the forest, allowing himself to become surrounded by pine and oak and beech. Somewhere a distance off, a woodpecker thrummed loudly at a tree, and this was the only sound Eduard could hear for several minutes.

The old man stood at the entrance to the cave and smiled quietly at Eduard as he looked around him, as if seeing the world for the first time. And then the old man disappeared into the darkness, leaving Eduard alone.

* * *

Sleep often came early in the evenings for them. They would light a fire in the constructed pit and watch the flames. Sometimes, they spoke to each other in their own languages, knowing the other could not understand. They told of their pasts, of their regrets and hopes for the future. When one of them laughed at a story, the other laughed, as well. Other times, they would simply watch the dancing flames between them before they settled themselves back for sleep.

Many nights, Eduard would lay awake, wondering where the old man came from and how he had found himself in the cave. Eduard would look across the fire at the old man and create stories of his life, some more elaborate than others; some mirrored Eduard's own life while others were in stark contrast, but always, there was hope in those stories that the old man would one day escape from the cave and find whatever it was he had been searching for.

From across the cave, with the blaze separating the two men, Eduard found himself studying the old man frequently. During those moments when he looked the old man over and knew that the old man was doing the same to him, Eduard noticed the smile that spread across the other's face, dark and wet from the absence of several teeth, and he realized how much he cared about the old man. Though Eduard had no memories of his own grandfathers, when he looked at the old man, he saw a face he imagined a grandfather to have.

Just before he fell asleep, the old man would turn his head in the glow of the fire and stifle a yawn, and then he would lay his head down. Eduard would do the same, and as he lay there, thinking about his own life—about his father and the farm and Loise and how he'd held her so tightly to him that last night—he would find that he was crying for all those things that were lost completely to him.

The Dead

Over the next several days, Eduard began to leave the cave more frequently and for longer periods of time. Some afternoons he would walk with the old man, neither of them speaking. One of them might point something out to the other: a berry plant, or the carcass of an animal picked clean by scavenger birds.

On those walks, Eduard would often gather a handful of rocks and stop every so often to throw one at a tree. Once, Eduard handed a rock to the old man, who took it and threw at the stump of a tree that had fallen long ago. They laughed when the throw missed the stump by several feet, and though Eduard offered the old man another rock, the latter simply smiled and shook his head.

The ninth day, Eduard and the old man walked farther away than they had in the previous week. The new landscape looked indistinguishable from other parts of the forest, and Eduard did not realize where they were until he smelled the odor. It was the sick sweet aroma of death he had come to know on the farm in his younger days. He let his eyes move over the area around them, trying to find the source of the smell. They walked on quietly, the old man showing no notice that anything was wrong. And then, without Eduard realizing it, they were at the clearing.

Scattered all about the area and out further into the surrounding forest were dead soldiers. The majority wore the gray uniforms of the *Wehrmacht*, the same that he still wore, though his was now filthy and ripping in several areas from where he'd moved over the cave floor. The other men in the clearing were dressed in the light olive brown uniform of the French.

Eduard felt bile rising in his throat, but he swallowed it down and coughed, partly at the smell and partly at the sight in front of him. Many of the corpses were without part of a leg or an arm. Others had bullet holes shot through their bodies, many with small entrances and large exploded exits where blood had spilled out of the wound.

Eduard separated from the old man and slowly walked forward; he had to turn his head from two men whose faces had been blown away to charred black bone from a grenade blast. Near the middle of the clearing, sitting by itself with nothing and no one else near it for several steps, was a black boot, the same kind as his own. Eduard bent down and held it. He expected a bloody foot to be inside, but the boot was empty, as if during the firefight someone had taken his boot off and thrown it into the air, as either a show of stubborn pride or an acceptance of defeat. It wasn't until that moment that Eduard wondered if he was not, in fact, the only member of his group to have survived. He wondered if there could be some other man who'd escaped the devastation simply wandering the French landscape with only one boot on.

Eduard turned to look at the old man, though the old man had left Eduard alone in the clearing, holding an orphaned boot and surrounded by dead men, many of whom Eduard had spoken with only days earlier.

That afternoon and into the evening, Eduard took a dozen trips back to the cave. He gathered different items from the clearing, items either fallen and scattered to the ground or things he took from out of different soldier's packs. He carried those items in armfuls back to the cave, where he set them down in the darkness and then returned to the clearing for more. This took him hours to complete, though he did not stop to rest or even take a drink from one of the many canteens he took from around soldiers' necks.

His hands shook each time he removed something from one of the men. Several times, he found himself crying at what he was doing and he needed to bend over, his hands on his knees, and breathe deeply. Before moving on, Eduard whispered words to the dead men, both of apology and of thanks.

By nightfall, he had stockpiled rifles and pistols, blankets and coats, shirts and socks and several extra pairs of boots, a compass and a bible and some notebooks. His last trip to the clearing that night, Eduard took up the radio pack that the captain and lieutenants had been using when the attack began and he also grabbed hold of the bag of supplies that the medic carried with him. Eduard slung these around his neck and slowly walked back in the direction of the cave.

Eduard let his feet wander from the path a bit and he found himself at a slow moving stream. He hadn't known that the water was there, but figured that this was where the old man got their water from. At the stream, Eduard knelt down and dipped his cramped hands into the cold of it. He cupped water onto his face and then poured some on the back of his neck so that his body tensed and his breathing shortened. Then he stood and shouldered the bags and made his way to the cave, where he sloughed the packs off and sat in front of the fire and drank down the bowl of watery soup the old man handed him.

Eduard couldn't sleep that night. In the cracks of the burning wood he could again hear the gunshots from where he hid within the trees, and in the dying flames he could feel the life as it left the bodies of those men he had been surrounded by.

He rolled over and faced away from the flames, away from where the old man slept, but still he could not sleep, and so, instead, he walked outside the cave and sat on the dry ground just beside the entrance and listened to the sounds of the night; birds called out to each other in low, haunting voices, and small animals moved quickly around the forest, chasing and catching insects, who chirped and hummed and buzzed in the darkness. As he sat there, Eduard wondered how any person truly existed in a world so big as the one in which he lived.

In the early hours of the next morning, when the sun's light was beginning to stretch the shadows of trees westward, Eduard made his way back to the clearing.

He kept his eyes trained on the forest floor, neither listening to the scurry of animals nor feeling the cold of the morning on his face. His mind played over the conversations he'd had with the men whose bodies he was walking back to revisit. In morning hours, before they set out toward the next village, they would exchange tales of their lives; it was during those moments that he learned of men's families, their dreams and their indiscretions. Of children and wives and lovers. All those things held secret within a man's mind.

One morning several months earlier, Henry Fischer spoke of his parents and how he had come to be an orphan years ago. He was six then. "My father died in the war," Henry said. "And when my mother was told of his death, she walked out the door of our home, leaving my sister Margo and myself at the table where we were eating supper. We didn't know anything of where she had gone until the next afternoon, when Mr. Müller found her floating along the banks of the river. She'd drowned herself and left the two of us behind. Like we didn't matter to her at all." Henry spoke these last words in a voice little more than a whisper, yet what surprised Eduard even more than the story or the man's honesty was how Henry spoke these words without any emotion. No pain, no sorrow. It was as if he had accepted those events of his past. In that moment, as Eduard studied Henry in the new day's light, he realized that the latter had found the only way a person can continue to exist within the world: to numb yourself of everything around you.

That morning all those months ago, Eduard had wanted to ask Henry what he hoped for after the war was over, though he did not. Rather, he only nodded and then turned away from the other man, focusing his attention, instead, on a group of soldiers several steps away who were laughing at some story one of them was telling. Now, as Eduard walked through the forest toward the clearing, knowing that he would discover Henry's body amongst the others, he felt a strange relief at having refrained from asking the question.

There was a quiet that seemed to have settled over the clearing that morning, and Eduard wondered if the animals and birds were silent in some kind of respect for the pain and hurt of the place and what had happened there.

He walked slowly around the area, taking note of the different attitudes of the fallen men: some looked to have continued running even after they had been shot, their hands tightened to fists, their legs spread and bent at the knees, while others looked as if they had been arranged in a specific form, their arms crossed over their chests like they would for a church funeral. Along the edges of the clearing, Eduard noticed that some of the men were without skin on parts of their bodies and faces, their hands gnawed off from wolves and other scavenger animals that had come through earlier.

Eduard stopped beside one of the bodies and knelt down. He reached out and gently laid his hand out and felt the rigid muscles and taught skin beneath the gray clothing. The man had once been Hans Kreuger, but was now a corpse fallen in the middle of a clearing, and Eduard wondered what news would come to the boy's parents, and when. Would a soldier appear on the doorstep of the Kreuger's home and tell his mother and father what had happened? And how would his mother receive the news? Would she turn and fall into the arms of her husband, sobbing tears that would not stop until the day she, herself, died? Was there any way to accept the death of a child? Of anyone?

The sun was beginning to make its way into the eastern sky when Eduard stood. He walked several steps and then turned to look again at the silent boy again. He went back.

Without realizing what he was doing, Eduard knelt back down and then sat on the ground beside Kreuger's body. Around him were ferns, and on several of the ferns he could make out caterpillars and other small insects crawling on the green leaves. Eduard lay himself down so that he was flat on his back and then he closed his eyes. He could feel the bodies of the men surrounding him, as if there were some electric current that moved from their bones and their skin over the ground to where he was, and he dug his fingers into the black-turned soil, imagining what it must feel like to be one of those men.

Eduard stayed like this for several hours, though he could not tell how much time actually had passed. He was imagining the lives of the men around him, creating fictions for each of them: those things they would do when they returned home, after the war had finished. For most of the men, both German and French, he gave them names and features. There was Peter, a French soldier who grew his beard long to cover the scars on his face so as not to scare his five-year-old daughter when she ran through the front door at full speed toward him, her bare feet almost slipping out on the gravel that lined the road. The way she embraced him. The way this man lifted his daughter into the air and twirled around with her, thinking to himself that if he never had to let go of her, if he could only stay in this one single moment for the rest of his life, that he would be happy. But this man did not exist, and this moment would never come to pass.

And then Eduard's mind moved beyond those fantasies and he was brought back to the world as it was. He found himself wondering what would come of these men's bodies. Would their forms calcify, creating in them stones that, over time, passersby would glance at and then move past without second thought? Would these men become sucked into the ground, become roots, jagged and gnarled, jut forth in places from the earth?

When Eduard opened his eyes again, he saw that the sun had moved so that it was directly above him. His head ached and he climbed slowly to his feet, making sure to catch his balance, which felt to him out of sorts. Near the western edge of the clearing, several packs, including his own, had been discarded in a pile. He walked over to them and took from one a short spade. From the look of the blade, it had only been used once or twice; the edges were still sharp, and there was a shine to the metal.

In the center of the clearing, a few steps away from the packs, Eduard thrust the blade into the ground and shoveled out a section of earth. He did this over and over, never stopping to think of what he was doing, never realizing that he was crying the whole while. Instead, he found himself concentrating on the work, the constant movement of his arms, the grip of his hands around the tool.

On the ground a short distance away from him, Eduard saw a crucifix; the chain that it was attached to had been broken and it lay half-covered with dirt. He stopped digging. Some man among the many around him had worn that crucifix, believing that it would protect him. But it had not. Eduard wondered at how God could watch his own creations kill each other in hate, and he looked around him, noticing once again the ways in which the men's bodies lay. There was no reason, no purpose that he could understand.

Was this God's doing? He shook his head at the question and then began digging again.

Over the afternoon, blisters formed on his fingers and his palms, and his back tightened and hurt, though he would not quit until he had dug a grave large enough to bury each of the men around him. Both German and French buried together, he decided, for in death there is no difference among men.

Stories

It took him nearly five days to bury all of the men. While he worked, he constantly moved his eyes across the forest, looking for other soldiers, either German or French, but he was alone. Wherever the war was being fought, it had moved on from this place and left him behind.

During those evenings, he walked back to the cave slowly; his arms and legs coated in dirt and mud, his face streaked a darker skin. Beneath his pants and shirt, his body was filmed over with sweat, and even though he stopped at the creek and held his hands under for upwards of fifteen minutes, there remained a stain on his fingers and on his palms that he could not wash away.

With his hands held under the water, Eduard would pick off the strings of skin around the blisters that had developed. When he finished with his hands, he would dip his head under, letting his breath catch in his chest and come out in strained, short bursts, bubbled in the water. Then he'd stand and walk back to the cave.

On those nights, the old man could smell death on Eduard's skin, though he made no mention of it, in neither his language nor any other. He simply carried a bowl of watery soup over to Eduard and nodded to him while he ate.

Before he rolled the men in the grave, Eduard searched them for anything of value. Over each man, he said a silent word of farewell. Even if they could not hear his words, Eduard thought, at least he could hear the words and know that each man was sent away from this world with some moment of kindness, however short that moment might be.

When he finished, Eduard covered the men with dirt. He did not stop until the men disappeared and all that was left was a long patch of ground whose soil had recently been upturned, though no man could ever guess at the reason.

And then he left the clearing and headed back to the cave and to the old man.

In the cave, Eduard took stock of the items he'd collected. From a distance, the old man watched him, and even though Eduard could not see the other in the darkness of the cave, he imagined that the old man was, for some reason, content.

By the time Eduard finished, there was a stack of a dozen or so blankets, seven canteens, twenty boxes of matches, a gas mask, numerous jackets of varying sizes, two shovels, four metal bowls, four pairs of boots, the radio pack that no longer worked, and a pile of bibles with different names inscribed on the covers or handwritten on the inside page with well wishes from parents and grandparents.

Beside these items, Eduard sat and thumbed through a small leather book that he found in the pocket of one of the French soldiers. Tucked within the center of the book was a small photograph of a girl, maybe twenty-years-old. She was sitting on a white divan, her hair in curls. In the photo, her eyes shown dark, and Eduard found his gaze drifting constantly back to her eyes, as if she were looking directly at him through time and space. On the back of the photo was a note in pencil, hardly legible now with most of the graphite having been rubbed off from the amount of times the photo had been taken out and looked at and then replaced. Eduard imagined the French soldier lying on the hard earth, a blazing fire beside him; Eduard watched in his mind the way the man took the photo from the book, looking around as he did so to ensure that no one else was paying him attention, so that he would be alone in this moment with the image of his love, that they would be together despite the distance. And it was this moment, which took place within Eduard's mind, that was the last time the young soldier and the girl would ever spend together.

The book itself was a journal that the soldier had kept. The pages had been scrawled over with a pencil in a loose, sloppy hand. Eduard spoke no French, and so he sounded the letters of the words out as best he could, but he did not know what story was told there. He read the book in its entirety this way, a spoken tribute of sorts to the dead man. Evenings, Eduard would take up the small black book, look at the photo of the girl, stare into her dark eyes for a moment, and then read a page. When he finished, Eduard created the story anew in his own language. Many nights, the story focused on the girl from the photo, of how she and the French soldier had met and of her affections for him. Other nights, Eduard created the story of the man's family and his youth, of the early hours the man would wake so as to watch the sun's rise over the crops of the farm. Eduard never realized that he was speaking his own history through this other man's life.

Winters

Time seemed a fiction within the cave.

Occasionally airplanes streaked across the sky, and if Eduard was inside the cave when he heard the heavy scream of the engines, he would run outside and look up to where the sound was coming from. He'd watch as the planes became specks in the horizon. It was only in those brief moments when he shielded his eyes from the glare of the sun and watched the black dots disappear along with the echo of their presence that Eduard was reminded that he and the old man were not alone in the world. That they had not been forgotten by God or whatever other being it was that controlled the goings on of life.

In the mornings, when Eduard or the old man left the cave to gather food or water or to relieve themselves outside, they would move slowly, peeking their head into the cool air and looking around at the forest about them before exiting completely. Though neither spoke it aloud, they each felt the fear of walking out and being surrounded by one nation's soldiers, whether German or French or some other invading country's.

There were times when the sound of a snapped branch made them freeze within the cave. They would strain their ears toward the sound, keeping as still as their bodies allowed them. In their chests, their hearts beat heavily in rhythm to one another. Several minutes would pass in this manner, the two men mannequins, preparing for their cave home to be invaded by men whose faces they could not see and whose language they could not understand. But this never happened. Instead, the noises from outside the cave were simply the natural world's way of speaking comfort to them.

Within the cave, a fire burned every night and settled to embers during the days, though occasionally, especially during winter days when the world outside the cave was covered in white snow, the fire would burn constantly, and the two men, covered over in blankets and jackets, would huddle close to the flames to keep warm.

During the first year there, Eduard walked around the forest, setting traps for small animals every morning. He remembered the farm and his father teaching him about different types of traps. He had been seven years old then, and his father led him out into the field to where rabbits had destroyed a small section of the crops. "Need to fix this," his father said, "And you're going to help me." Eduard smiled at the memory, remembering how his father had guided his small hands, helping him to tie different knots in ropes to fashion into various types of snares.

Each evening, Eduard walked to the different locations and collected whatever bounty had been caught. If the animal was still alive, he'd crush its head in with a stone. Though he carried a pistol at his hip, Eduard dared not fire it for fear of what unwanted attention the sound might draw, from beast or, worse, man. If one of the traps had caught an animal or been tripped by a falling branch, Eduard would reset the trap and then move on to the next one. After he stopped at each trap, Eduard would bring the small bodies back to the cave.

The old man would take the animals and skin them. Then he'd skewer pieces of meat with long sticks he had collected long ago, and the two of them would sit beside the fire slowly turning their sticks in their hands until the meat began to sizzle and brown. Then they ate, their chins becoming slick from the grease and fat of the food.

As the winter months approached, the focus became not so much collecting food but collecting wood. When the forest trees became completely vacant of leaves, Eduard would wander the woodlands for hours, stopping back intermittently to drop off armloads of wood he'd collected. The old man would then organize the wood into stacks against the cave wall. This wood they tried to keep from burning until they needed it. Instead, Eduard would go out in the early mornings, before the sun had risen, and he would pull branches from the trees. These branches he would bring back and place beside the burning fire to dry out. When these branches were put on the blaze, they would elicit heavy black smoke, and Eduard and the old man would cough at the smell of it and wave their arms about them to try and remove the haze from their faces.

During winter, they drank water from melted snow and ice that Eduard collected from the creek. They grew thin. Every few days, Eduard, covered in three jackets, would hike out in the snow with the shovel in his hand. He'd make his way to various trees in the forest and then dig the blade into the hard-crusted earth, breaking through the snow and ice, eventually coming to the roots of the tree. He would hammer away at the roots, peeling off strips and putting them in his pocket. Then he would jam the shovel blade into the bark of the tree, gouging out portions with the metal until larger chunks of wood broke away and fell to the ground. These he would pick up and store away in his pocket with the strips of roots.

Every few days, Eduard would walk by some of the plants around the forest; he'd clear away the snow and then move his hand over the brittle leaves and branches and then reach further inside, looking for any trace of color, red or blue or purple, to show through. Occasionally, he'd find some frozen berries, and these he would pick. Though he was always tempted to eat one or two, Eduard always carried them back to the cave and handed them over to the old man, who would boil the roots and bark and few berries in the metal bowl, and the two of them would take a deep sip from before passing it back to the other man.

Rarely in the winter would Eduard find an animal on his scavenging trips, though when he did, he would take from his pocket the pistol and steady his hands before pulling the trigger. From inside the cave, the old man would hear the pistol shot and know that he would be eating meat that night, and he smiled at the thought while he waited for Eduard to come back.

Out of the Trees

It was late spring when she appeared.

The evening sun was low in the western skyline as she emerged from the cluster of beech trees. When he saw her, Eduard dropped the two rabbits he was carrying and moved himself quickly behind the nearest tree. He pulled out the pistol and held it at his side. His hand was shaking, and he felt shivers course over his body, along his limbs and his back and continue up the nape of his neck.

Eduard took a deep breath to steady himself and then slowly peeked around the tree and watched her, studying the woman for any indication that she had seen him, though she gave no hint and he doubted he had been found out, as she was still a distance away.

She moved in a drunken stagger, as if her legs were made of a heavy metal. Her feet were bare of any shoes, and he watched as she moved in and out of the shadows from the trees above and around her. Her head was down, her gaze directed to her feet, as if she were studying the earth that surrounded her as she walked.

Sweat beaded along his hair line and his cheeks felt hot under his beard as he watched her move closer to where he hid. He tightened his grip on the pistol and was about to raise it when she fell. She did not get up. Eduard watched her where she lay, his eyes, every several seconds, lifting from her form and moving over the landscape around him in search of some sign that this was a trap, that he was being watched. After several minutes like this, he emerged from behind the tree and walked slowly over to her. He trained the pistol on her the whole while. It wasn't until he came within a step or two of her that he noticed the condition she was in. Eduard looked once more around the forest before pocketing the pistol and bending down to lift her from the ground. Her eyes opened briefly when he settled her body in his arms, but then her eyes closed again and she fell asleep while he carried her back to the cave.

In the flickering light of the fire, he studied her. Even in sleep, there was a strange restlessness to her face, the way her fingers twitched spastically in her dreams and then settled themselves without reason. Her body was darkly textured in mud and filth, and he wiped her face clean with a cloth wetted with his saliva.

A moment later, the old man brought over a bowl of water and left in on the ground beside where Eduard sat. He gently patted Eduard on the back and then moved off to the other side of the cave and sat down and opened a book he'd taken from the stack that Eduard had collected from the dead.

Eduard reached out and touched her hand. It felt hot and sticky with sweat. Then he brought his hand to her forehead and felt the fever there. He looked over to the old man and saw the latter nod his head at him.

Though he was afraid of waking her, Eduard knew she needed to be rid of her wet clothing, and so he slowly unbuttoned the coat she wore. He guided her arm gently through the sleeve, and then the other. Beneath the coat, she wore a white shirt of thin material that had been soaked through with sweat or snow so that the indentation of her navel, the small brown of her nipples, showed through slightly. He felt his breath catch when he saw her skin through the material, and he turned once again to the old man but the latter was no longer there.

Eduard went to fetch one of the extra blankets that had been stacked against the wall of the cave. He sat back down beside her. His hands shook in hesitation and fear as he reached out and lifted the shirt from off the woman, cradling her head in his hand while he did so. He could feel the susurrations of life within her. The grime of her hair, the movements of dream motion in her neck all painted her as some strange beast he knew nothing of. Eduard sat her up, cradling her head against his chest as he spread the blanket on the rock beneath her, and then he laid her back down.

Deep purple bruises stretched up the length of her arms. Scarred marks circled her wrists and her shoulders. He bent closer to examine these wounds. After several seconds, she turned her head in her sleep, and then settled her body peacefully.

Eduard felt her bare stomach with the back of his hand, feeling the heat there. He dipped the cloth into the bowl of water and then rung it out. Then he laid the cloth on her stomach. Water rolled slowly down the contours of her skin, gliding around invisible hair and eventually falling to the blanket to disappear in the fabric there. After a minute or so, he lifted the cloth and wetted it anew and then laid it on a different part of her body. He repeated this act over and over countless times that first night. There was no expression on his face as he dipped the cloth and rung it out and then replaced it on her body, no joy nor pain; from an outsider, it would have looked as if he were a penitent performing some ritual of forgiveness for a sin he was unaware of having committed.

After a while, Eduard covered the woman with another blanket and then moved several steps away. He lay down on the hard stone and watched her. And he continued to watch her until the old man came back into the cave and laid down a distance off from where she slept. Eduard continued to watch her into the middle hours of the night, listening to the sound now of two other breaths alongside his in the darkness of the cave. And he watched her until his own eyes closed in sleep.

Awake

When Eduard entered the cave, he was carrying several rabbits he'd collected from the traps that afternoon. The fire was burning brightly, and in the darkness he saw the shadow of the old man seated up against the far wall, leafing through one of the bibles. Eduard often found the old man in that position, looking at words foreign to him in the half light. Only once did Eduard ask the old man what he was reading. The old man simply looked up and smiled and then nodded as if in agreement to something Eduard had said, and then he turned his attention back to the book.

Eduard walked over to the fire pit and sat on the cold floor, across from where the woman still slept in the position he left her an hour earlier. He took up his knife and began to carve the skin and fur free from the rabbits, letting the warm blood drip onto the dark stone between his legs. After several cuts with the knife, he pulled the skin free from the body, feeling the rip of the sinewy tendons. He dropped the pieces of skin beside him and then set to work stripping the meat from the bone; these pieces he set in a small earthen bowl the old man had found in the forest several years earlier. In a short while, the old man would come over and they'd skewer the meat with sticks and roast the food over the flames. Eduard finished with the first rabbit and then picked up the next and began to carve away at the skin. Occasionally, he found himself glancing up to where the woman lay, but he quickly looked away, feeling a strange guilt as he did so.

As he worked at the rabbits, his hands becoming coated in blood and viscera, sweat beginning on the back of his neck, he found himself thinking of her.

By what means had she ended up in the cave? Her story or her body's conflicts were mysteries to which he had no answers. What paths wound about so that she came to lay across from him? And what things could she tell him of the darknesses of the world? Those things he knew nothing of. Though he had seen what men were capable of doing to one another in battle, this woman was something entirely different. He had his own demons, but he realized as he looked over at her and listened to her deep breaths, that there were others out in the world who were plagued by far worse devils than he knew. *Speak their name, relive that moment*, he thought, *and you are forever haunted by a power too strong to overcome.*

He finished with the rabbits and then moved over to where she lay. Her body was quiet, though every so often she allowed a glimpse into her world with a slight movement of her hand, a twitch of her head or leg. At times, a cry escaped her throat and echoed within the silent space they all three inhabited; those sounds seemed neither fully human nor animal, but of some creature in between. It was a sound created from within her dreams.

Eduard remembered his own dreams—of the farm and his father and Loise, of the ocean when he was a boy. In that moment, in the orange-red glow of the fire, the sleeping woman seemed at peace within the world, if even for the briefest of moments, and Eduard knew that there was some type of hope for her. And if there was hope for her, then there might also be hope for himself.

She slept for nearly two days. Eduard and the old man took turns watching over her. They dripped water into her mouth, moistening the dried and cracked lips. They replaced the blanket covering her every few hours.

When her eyes did open, she looked around the cave in confusion. She sat up slowly, and put her hand down on the cool stone to brace herself from her unsteadiness. Nausea passed through her stomach, and she turned to vomit but she was unable to and so she only coughed. The blanket that had been covering her naked skin fell off her shoulders and she reached up and pulled it tight to her body.

It wasn't until she tried to stand that she saw the two men, one young and one old, standing a distance off, watching her quietly. She screamed out in fear, pushing her body backward until she was stopped by the cave wall, unable to escape from whatever this place was.

The two men waved their hands at her; the old man issued a weak sounding *Shhh* while the young man spoke out loud. "It's all right," he said. "You're all right."

She shook her head and turned to stand again and run away, but her eyes and her body were too weak in that moment and she found that she could not move beyond a few feet. And so she fell down again and covered her face with her hands. She began to cry, and her body shook in convulsions that she could not calm. Though she didn't realize it, she repeated the same words over and over in a soft whisper. *I tried I tried.* Words to calm herself, lies to allow her to be at peace. Her body rocked back and forth, mucus and tears running down her lips and cheeks and chin. The blanket fell completely free from her body and in that moment she felt alone in the world, abandoned and lost.

A minute or so passed in this manner, and then she felt the blanket put back onto her shoulders. A scuffling sound came from out the darkness of her closed eyes, and when she opened them she saw him, the younger of the two men, kneeling several steps away. She pulled the blanket tightly to her and wiped her eyes with it. Even in the darkness of the place, she could see that the young man's body was thin and frail. Most of his face was covered in shadows, though every so often the firelight illuminated the surroundings long enough for her to see him clearly before he was cast back into shadows. His face was covered by a beard, and she could hardly see his eyes in the darkness of the place, but she did not feel fear in that moment.

As she looked at him, she wondered if she was merely dreaming, or if she had truly escaped and found some strange sanctuary.

Paintings

That night, the three of them sat around the fire pit.

It was late, and though the flames were tall and the heat strong an hour and a half earlier when they quietly cooked their food and ate, the fire had disappeared and all that was left were embers that gave off only a faint hint of light and warmth. Every so often, one of them took a drink of water from the tin cups that Eduard had collected years earlier. The smell of cooked rabbit still lingered around them like a phantom.

Their eyes moved about the dark regions of the cave; none of them wanted to look at the others. It wasn't until the old man shifted his body to stand and move off to his corner of the cave to sleep that she spoke.

Her name was Anais, she told them.

She spoke German, though Eduard could hear an accent to it.

"My mother was French, my father German," she said quietly, after he asked.

Eduard nodded his head in understanding, as if all of his questions were settled in those few words.

Silence fell between the three of them again.

From deep within the cave, the trickle of water seemed to grow louder, and outside the cave's mouth crickets and other bugs spoke to the world around them in supplication to their god. This sound, of nature continuing on, acted as a lullaby, and each of them found their eyes gently closing, until all three of them were asleep.

Anais quickly came to understand the workings of her strange new existence. She spent much of her time those first days watching the other two men, trying to better understand who they were and what they truly wanted. Yet even after days of studying their movements, their routines, the ways they spoke, not to each other but rather to themselves—short conversations and questions that may or may not have had any answers—she could understand no more about them than she had when she first awoke to the two of them standing there a distance off, watching her.

During the first several weeks, she stayed with the old man while Eduard went off to check on his traps and gather wood. He left twice a day: once in the morning, just after he woke, and again in the evening, as the sun was setting.

The old man occupied his time by sitting alone in the farther reaches of the cave: those places she dared not journey into. Every hour or so, he came over to check on the fire, sometimes adding new logs to the blaze to keep it from burning too low. After he did so, he walked back to the far side of the cave, away from where Anais sat. At times, she saw the old man writing in a book. He'd look up and see her watching him, and he would quickly close the book and tuck it away in the pocket of his pants. She wondered what confessions might be written on those pages, what story might be told, though she would never ask and he would never offer.

There were times in those early weeks when Anais would watch Eduard come in from one of his journeys to the outside world. He'd set down whatever small animal he found in the traps and then he would walk over to the collection of supplies against the wall. There, Eduard would bend down and pick something up and then, without slowing his step, he'd walk into the dark depths of the cave. Anais would watch as he faded from sight, and he would not return from these trips for upwards of an hour.

After a month of watching him move off into the darkness, Anais stopped him while he walked over to the supplies and asked if she could come. These were the first words she'd spoken since the night she told her name. He had wanted to speak to her, ask her a question and hear her answer, but he was too afraid of the silent reply, and so he kept those questions buried away in his mind.

Many nights, Eduard fell asleep to the sounds of hushed sobs coming from where she slept, and though he wanted to offer her some comfort, to place his hand upon hers, smile and tell her that everything would be all right—whatever that might mean—he simply closed his eyes tighter until he found himself caught within the trap of his dreams, both those of reality and those of hope.

"Can I come?" she asked.

He nodded his head, though he remained silent.

She stood up, feeling the tightness in her legs loosen, and then followed as Eduard walked over to the supplies and picked something up from between two blankets.

He looked over to see that she was standing beside him. "Come on," he whispered, and then he turned and began to walk into the darkness of the cave.

She looked back only once to see the old man sitting beside the fire, his head cradled in his hands as he stared at the flames, watching them dance upward until they disappeared into the air.

They walked for a long time. Eduard told her early on to duck her head low and drag the fingers of her right hand against the side of the cave so as to guide her. Their steps were slow, and the sound of rocks scraping together under their feet seemed to grow louder the farther they went. After a while more, the steady trickling sound of water that she listened to so intently back where they came from became deeper and heavier, and Anais wondered if they would come across a river within the cave, wondered if she would simply walk from out the air into the water and be carried away to some different place, where there was no more darkness or fear or pain. But that did not happen. Instead, they simply continued on.

Eventually, Eduard stopped walking. "Okay," he said, and though he whispered the word, his voice seemed to echo all around.

The two of them stood in the complete darkness for several seconds.

"Look at your hands," he said, and she did, though she could see nothing in front of her but blackness.

Eduard listened to her breathing, listened as it slowed and quieted. "I was terrified to come in here," he said. "I thought of the ghosts and demons that might live here. But then I realized there were no such things outside of us and what we do to each other."

She turned around slowly, looking to see if there was any glint of light behind her, any indication of where she might be, but there was nothing outside the voice that spoke now to her and to the darkness. Cold air moved all around her, tossing her hair gently around her face, causing her to brush loose strands from out of her eyes.

"It took me nearly two and a half years to come into the dark. I started slow, going only so far that I could still see the fire burning, but then I moved on a little more and a little more, each time moving deeper in than I was before." His voice became quieter, a whisper whose echo sounded more like the wind than human speech. "This, right now, is the farthest I've ever been."

She didn't realize she had spoken until she heard her voice repeat itself back to her. "I can't go outside the cave. I've tried, when you're out there getting food, but I can't."

"It's okay."

She was quiet for a minute. "Is it?"

"It is."

There was silence for a while.

"Why do you come here?" she asked

"To know that I'm not alone."

"How?"

"I'll show you."

There was a slight clicking sound and then the entire space around them was thrown into light. Anais closed her eyes quickly and brought her hand up to block her face. "It's okay," he said. She opened her eyes slowly, squinting and seeing that Eduard held in his hand a small cigarette lighter. The flame was low, though in its glow she saw that she was closer to Eduard than she knew.

In the dull yellow-orange of the light, she looked at him and he at her. His hair was long, stretching several inches past the collar of his shirt; some of it fell onto his shoulders. His beard was also longer than she had originally thought.

Eduard smiled slightly at her, seeing that she was not as old as he'd first guessed. She might only have been twenty years old. Her hair looked to have once been a light brown but had since turned a darker color from the dirt and mud that were tangled within it. A cut ran across the left side of her face, down from her cheek to her jawline and then up a short distance in the direction of her ear.

After several seconds, Eduard moved his eyes away from her face. He looked at something behind her. "There," he said and nodded his head for Anais to follow his gaze.

She turned. Her breath caught for a second in her throat before she could breathe deeply in, and he remembered that he had had the same reaction the first time.

The cave wall was covered in various drawings of different colors and sizes—drawings that detailed the stories of some indigenous people who had all been forgotten, save for this strange record of their existence. These images stretched along the wall as far as Anais could see in the light.

"I come here to know that I'm not alone," Eduard said. "It shows me that someone else lived here too. There's some comfort in that, I think." His eyes moved over the wall and the hints of a smile grew on his face while he held the lighter higher so as to see more clearly the images nearer the cave's ceiling.

Anais walked a step closer to the wall and stretched out her hands to touch the cold stone. She moved her palms over the pictographs, covering and then uncovering images of suns and ships and soldiers, of heroes and slaves and conquerors and the conquered people, and of beasts and monsters painted there in blacks and reds and blues. A little farther down was a section of wall taller than two men and stretching the length of five or six steps completely full of images of birds. Some were in flight while others were sitting perched on invisible tree branches, and still others stood on legs too thin.

Anais turned back to look at Eduard, but she saw that he was not paying attention to her. Instead, his eyes were moving over the images, as if trying to remember each one, as if these images could unlock some mystery he'd been contemplating. She turned back and looked at the wall again, wondering what story was being told and by what people.

And in that moment, as she heard Eduard's calm breaths beside her and her eyes swam across the images left by men or women a millennia ago, she felt hopeful and at peace.

After several more seconds, Eduard took his thumb from the lighter and the cave descended to complete darkness once again.

"We need to save the flame for next time," he said, and Anais couldn't help but to hear the first word in that sentence and smile at it.

Embers

During the days, the three of them lived in silence, often going full mornings and afternoons without uttering a single word to one another, but they made up for this in the evenings.

When they ate their dinners, the only sounds were the pop of sap in the fire and the occasional slurp of water from one of them as they drank. After they finished their food, though, they exchanged stories, all fictions either fashioned during the day as they went about their lonely activities or made up in the moment. Even the old man told his own fantastic tales, though neither Eduard nor Anais could understand his speech. They would instead watch as the old man's face contorted in grimace or smile and listen to the way his voice changed pitch and volume. In their minds, they created their own stories to the ones the old man told, their own translations of his.

The three often found themselves laughing at each other. Tears would roll down their faces as they laughed, and they would not wipe these tears away, as these moments allowed them to forget their pasts, for the only way to make sense of the world and all of its cruelty and hate is through the stories we tell and the stories we're told. And though they could not understand how, their words carried within them a kind of magic: words tasted when spoken, slipping from out their mouths like slurred speech over a drunken tongue, so that there was often more truth in these words than in the whole of their dreams or their thoughts throughout the days.

As the weeks passed, their stories became more elaborate as they each tried to best the others. They told of princes and dragons, flowers that sang to the wind, and birds who flew the entire earth over to find their lost loves. Kingdoms that rose and fell within a day. But there was love always at the heart of each story: lovers who ended their lives together, holding each other's hand tightly within their own; lovers who ran away from the world, leaving behind them all the pain they'd ever known.

This was how they lived, in those few moments each night, gathered around the fire, with their images dancing on the cave walls all around them like some quiet shadowplay to which there was no beginning and would be no end.

And after they finished, they'd slowly lay back and make themselves comfortable on the stone floor.

Anais would often stay awake for hours into the night, watching as the flames died down. She would look over to where Eduard slept and she'd smile knowing that he was there, only a short distance away. There was a strange sense of wonder for her in this place, something she could not understand, and she did not want to. And as she lay there in the firelight, she'd think to herself that the waking world was better than the dreams she had, and so she'd tell herself to stay awake for just a little while longer.

From Below

Several months after she came to stay with them in the cave, Eduard asked Anais to come with him to check for food. They would only be gone an hour, he said to her. She looked up from where she sat next to the fire, smiled slightly at him, and then nodded. "Yes," she said and set down the book she had been reading.

It was cold outside the cave. The days were getting shorter with the coming winter—her first one spent in the cave. Already, the trees had shed most of their leaves.

"In the morning," Eduard said, "the ground is hard with frost. Beneath your step, you can feel the crack of the earth." He looked over and smiled at her.

Anais pulled the heavy coat tight around her. She noticed how Eduard walked slowly. There was a limp in his step that she had not noticed before and she wondered if he had always been this way, or if he had recently hurt himself, though she did not ask. Instead, she tried her best to match her step to his, so that their footsteps fell at the same time.

After several minutes of walking in silence, they came to the first stop. She stayed several steps away while Eduard walked over to the base of a tree and cleared the area of twigs and leaves he'd used to disguise the trap.

This was the first time she'd been outside the cave since Eduard found her staggering through the forest. She shivered at the cold and at the memory that had brought her to this place. Her eyes moved over the gray world that surrounded her; as if for the first time, Anais took note of the trees, thin and jagged, that kept the rest of the world away.

Eduard covered the trap again and walked toward her, empty handed. He shook his head as if in answer to some question that she had not spoken, and then he continued on to the next trap, leaving her to catch up to him.

As they walked, Anais could not help but notice the silence in the forest. Apart from their footsteps, she could hear no other animal or bird. Not even the flow of water, and she wondered if this was the sound, now, of her life, of her world. She looked over at Eduard and saw his eyes quickly move away from where he had been watching her.

"What were you reading?" he asked.

"What?"

"The book from inside. What was it?"

She looked down at the ground; pine needles and leaves soggy and crumpled created a path for her to walk. "It was about a boy and girl who fall in love. Their families hate one another, though."

"*Romeo and Juliet*?"

Anais looked up and nodded. "Yes," she said. In the several seconds she was looking down, the world around her darkened from the coming evening.

"Have you read it before?"

She shook her head. "No."

Eduard smiled and gave a soft laugh.

"What?" she asked.

"I've read that so many times."

"You have?"

"My father handed me a book of plays when I was young; I spent every night reading from it. I fell asleep to those words. My favorite of Shakespeare's, though, is *King Lear*."

"I've never heard of it."

Eduard slowed his walk and looked over at Anais. "We'll have to fix that."

She looked over at him, noticed the kindness in his face, the seriousness there. "I'd like that," she said.

It took them an hour and a half to check the traps, much longer than Eduard normally took, and she didn't know if that was because of her, or whether he had simply slowed his pace to enjoy the world around him.

By the time they reached the cave again, night had completely fallen. If she had been out there alone, she would never have been able to find the cave, as each tree and hillside blended into the darkness of the land.

Anais was about to duck her head down and walk inside when she turned around and saw Eduard several steps away; he was looking up at the stars and what moon there was. In the hazy moonlight, he looked to be a black silhouette set out against the blue-dark background of the world around him. He stood there, not moving, holding the four squirrels that he'd collected from the last several traps they visited.

She was worried to speak aloud, afraid to break Eduard of whatever moment it was he was lost within, but she couldn't simply leave him there alone either. After several seconds of watching him, she spoke. "Are you all right?" she asked. Her voice cracked, as if she hadn't used it in months.

He broke from his trance and looked at her. "Come with me," he said, and he reached his hand out in her direction.

Eduard led her to a small clearing not far away from the cave, barely big enough for four people to sit.

They lay on their backs several feet from each other, their arms and legs spread apart, as if they were reaching with each limb as far as they could to the ends of the forest.

"This is where I come to think and be alone."

"I can go back, if you want to be by yourself," she responded, but he stopped her.

"I don't want to be," he said.

Above them now was the night sky, spread out for them to witness, to breathe in like some scent blowing along in the wind. They were surrounded by trees whose finger-like branches stretched out above them, intersecting and then separating. To Anais, the branches looked like a spider's web, and she felt in that moment as if she were the insect caught within the web's hold, though this did not frighten her.

The sliver of moon glowed above them. Eduard had positioned himself so that one of the trees was blocking the moon from his view. From this angle, an aura of moonlight haloed the dark outline of the tree, making it look to him as if the tree was glowing from its edges.

On evenings like this, Eduard found himself thinking about the past.

His voice was soft when he spoke to her, and until Eduard heard her reply he wondered if he had spoken the words aloud at all. "Do you think there are sins in this world you can't be forgiven of?"

Anais had not expected Eduard to speak. She had, instead, been feeling her toes slowly going numb in the cold, her fingertips beginning to pulse. When he finished his question, she thought and then answered, her own voice little more than a whisper. "No. I can't believe that. There has to be forgiveness."

Eduard was silent for several seconds. Then he spoke again. "Even for those things in this world we've done?"

"I believe it," she whispered.

"Then how are you forgiven of those things?" There was pain in his voice that she could hear. It sounded as if he were about to weep.

Anais turned her head so that she looked in his direction. Even with the shadows from the branches, she could see his face. He was looking over at her. Her eyes focused on his, and she noticed the gentle shine of them in the moonlight. If she stared long enough, would she be able to see into the hidden parts of his soul?

Eduard asked again, this time even quieter, so that the word sounded more like a gentle breeze than human speech. "How?"

"Love," she said, finally. "You love in return for the things you've done. And for the things you've seen."

The Farm

For Eduard, there was a magic to the land and to the farm, something that could not be gotten rid of, no matter the distance he traveled away. It breathed continually through all time, becoming a part of him, an ancestor more real than even blood could define.

He was raised on the land. As a child, he woke with his father before the sun's rise, and the two of them would walk out into the field and begin the day's work. How many sunrises had Eduard watched from that field? Watch as the blanket of night would lift slowly from the crops and the golden wheat and barley would glow in the morning light, becoming aflame with the sun. "Each time, it's like seeing it for the first," his father often said, and Eduard could think of no description more accurate.

After his father died, though, he could no longer watch the sun's rise from the field. He was reminded too much of his father in those moments, and so he found his feet carrying him in the darkness of early morning to the river a mile or so away. There, he would sit on the banks and look out at the movement of the water. His thoughts often drifted to his father during those moments, and he'd wonder at what his father would think of him.

Eduard's mother died giving birth to him, and as far back as he could remember, his world consisted only of his father and himself. The two of them would spend all day in the field and then come back to the house in the evenings when the sun set. There, they would listen to the radio and eat their meal in silence. The only times Eduard could remember his father smiling were during nights, when the two of them sat beside the fire and listened to the news of the world.

He was seventeen when his father died, and he buried him beside his mother. On that afternoon, Eduard swore to himself that he too would be buried there, but this, like so many other promises in life, was a lie.

Most nights in the cave, Eduard found himself dreaming of the farm. Often it was of some obscure memory from his childhood that he'd not thought of in years: some afternoon when his father walked over to him in the field and patted him on the shoulder, or the sound of the insects outside as he fell asleep in his small bed while his father's snores came from down the hall. When he woke from those dreams, Eduard could still smell the soil, wet from the morning fog, and his hands felt dry and rough, as if he'd just come in from the field.

It was in those minutes after these dreams that Eduard wondered about the world in which he was living. He'd look up at the darkness of the cave's ceiling, search the shadows for reason, replaying memories from the day previous as if to assure himself that he was not dead. That the cave was not his afterlife.

Eduard met Loise five years after his father died.

She worked at the market. Once a week, Eduard would walk the four miles to the village to buy whatever necessities—bread and meat—he needed.

Over the weeks, their brief greetings expanded to short conversations; on the walks back to the farm, Eduard found himself replaying their words in his mind, smiling the whole while, so that if anyone were to walk or ride by, they would have considered him nothing but a fool.

He learned about her in those brief moments each week. She told him that her father owned the market and that she had been working there as long as she could remember. She'd wanted to go to school as a child but her father refused, saying that he would rather have no daughter than one educated, and so she only knew simple arithmetic. She could hardly even write, she confessed. Eduard told her that he could teach her if she wanted, and she said she would.

After several months, they began to spend time together away from the market. Eduard's weekly trip to the village increased to three or four trips a week; often he would walk there in the blue of evenings after he finished with the fields; those trips, he would not reach the market until the pitch dark of night.

From a short distance, he would wait for the market's lights to go out. Loise would walk outside, carrying a small bag of food, and she'd join him. The two of them would go off to the edge of the village, just beyond where the lights from homes and other shops could reach, and they would find a place to sit. Loise would take the food from the bag, and the two would eat quietly. Neither needed to speak during those meals; instead, there was comfort in knowing that the other was there, just an arm's length away.

Eduard would walk her home on those nights, watching as she made her way up the path to the door. When she disappeared inside, he'd turn and walk back to the farm and to his own house, which seemed emptier than ever before.

A year after they began their nighttime meals, Eduard asked if she would marry him. She was just biting into a piece of bread when he asked. The question seemed to come from the ether, neither practiced nor expected. She spat the bread out and wiped her mouth with the back of her hand. When she looked at him, she saw a strange, almost comical terror on his face. Loise was silent for a moment, and then Eduard asked again, this time with more command of his voice.

"Yes," she said quietly. She smiled and moved closer to where he sat and brought her arms around him. He reached up with both his hands and touched her bare skin gently. This was the first time they had touched each other.

They were married on a Sunday afternoon in late March. The skies outside were storming. Her mother and father and young sister Ida were the only people in attendance. During the whole of the ceremony, her father's face never once moved to form a smile, and Eduard was unsure if the man disapproved of his daughter's groom or if he was just upset at having lost a worker for the market.

Eduard had attached a carriage to two of his horses, and he and Loise road back to the farm sitting beside each other in the cold afternoon. When they were a mile away, it began to rain on them. Eduard took his coat off and wrapped her in it, trying to cover her head, but by the time they arrived at the house, they were both soaked through.

In the entry of the house, they stripped off their clothing, giggling the whole time. Breaths short, skin cold. They stopped their laughter when they realized they were each standing naked in front of the other. Eduard quickly looked away, his cheeks blushing crimson. When he looked back at Loise, he saw that she had moved so that she was now standing less than a step away. He could feel her breath on his chest.

She reached her hand up and placed it gently on the side of his face. He bent his head so that his eyes were looking directly into hers, and then he kissed her, feeling the cool moisture of the rain on her lips. Her hand moved from the side of his face and down the length of his arms until she reached his hand. She directed his touch to her belly and then moved his hand upward. Then she touched his body, feeling the contours of his form, the tingle of his skin. They remained like this for a long time, kissing and exploring each other with their hands, neither thinking of their pasts nor of what the future might bring.

They had been married four months when Eduard woke in the middle of the night and felt the warm liquid beside him. At first, he thought he was simply dreaming of the ocean, as he often dreamed. It wasn't until he felt Loise's movements on the bed next to him and heard the sounds of discomfort coming from the darkness that Eduard understood that he was awake.

He quickly sat up and then went over to the table in the corner of the room and lit the lamp. When he turned back to the bed, he saw Loise laying there. She still had her eyes closed, but he could not tell whether or not she was asleep. He walked back over to the bed and saw that a small space beneath her was wet with blood. Loise gently rocked back and forth, her breathing sounding strained. Dark shadows swam along the walls around them from the lamp. He reached out with a shaking hand and touched her shoulder. Loise opened her eyes and tried to sit up quickly but was unable to.

"Help me up," she said, Eduard set the lamp down on the floor and then reached out to raise her so that she was sitting. She reached down beneath the blanket and brought her hand back up. In the dim of the lamp's light, they could both see the blood on her fingers. It looked black, shining slightly like metal in the dark.

"I'm getting the doctor," he said, and turned to leave the room, but he was stopped when she called out to him.

"Don't," she said. Her voice shook in fear. "It's okay. I'm okay."

He turned and looked at her, confused. "I have to go," he said.

"Stay with me. Please." Her voice shook in fear.

Eduard felt like vomiting. Beneath him, his legs were weak.

"Hold me," she said. "Until morning. Then go." He looked to the door and then back to her. "Please," she whispered. He took a deep breath and then walked over to the bed and sat slowly beside her.

She reached over and held his hand. "I'll be okay." Her voice had become a whisper. She leaned her head against his chest. "I promise."

Eduard sat beside her the rest of the night, holding her body close to his. She would sleep for a while and then wake, before falling back asleep. When she did wake, Eduard would reach over and run his fingers gently through her hair. "Shhh," he whispered to her. "It's going to be all right," he'd say over and over, though he did not know if it would.

In the early morning, just as the sun began to show outside the bedroom's window, Eduard rode one of the horses to the village to fetch the doctor.

By the time the two of them, Eduard and Dr. Braun, arrived at the house, Loise was dead; her body was still warm to the touch.

Later that morning, Dr. Braun told him that she would have died regardless of when he left, though Eduard could not keep himself from wondering what might have happened had he gone sooner.

Loise was buried in the church graveyard the next day. Afterward, Loise's mother hugged Eduard, crying into his chest for several seconds and saying her apologies—though he did not know who the apologies were directed to. Her father simply shook Eduard's hand and walked away without a word.

When he was left alone, Eduard sat beside the mound of dirt and the open grave and cried.

Over the next several months, he tried to lose himself in his work. He woke even earlier than he used to, though instead of walking down to the river Eduard made his way directly out to the field and began cutting down the wheat and barley, gathering it in bushels, stacking them up to be delivered. He stayed out late each night, working away at the crops, his movements guided simply by memory. Many nights he did not eat but, instead, walked into the kitchen and fell asleep at the table, where he stayed until the next morning only to wake and begin the work all over again.

He entered the bedroom only once after Loise died. The bed was still covered in the same sheets from that night; the blood on the fabric had turned brown over time, and there was a faint metallic smell in the air. Nights when Eduard did not fall asleep at the table, he slept on the floor of the front room. He would turn the radio on and close his eyes to the news of the country, to broadcast speeches made by Hitler. And though Eduard had no views of what the man spoke of, he could not deny his passion. It was a passion for life that Eduard felt completely drained of.

Each day Eduard worked in the field, he grew more and more uneasy of the place. He felt as if the land was cursed, haunted by ghosts. He wished so desperately to reach out and hold Loise, to look into her eyes as he did that first night with her, to apologize for not saving her. Often during those months after her death, Eduard found himself in the middle of the field with tears streaming down his cheeks and falling to the ground. Would those tears bear more pain and anguish on this land, like an unwanted crop? Was there any escape from the hurt? He wondered these things as he looked back on the memories of his father and of Loise. Of his mother, whom he knew so little about.

As short a time as he had with Loise, he wanted to relive each day, even the last, if needed, just so he could speak into her ear those words he had never been able to say before. Those sentences he could only now construct. But he could not, and he needed to accept this, in one way or another.

It was a Thursday morning that he left. He lit a fire in the hearth and then packed a small bag full of clothes and some food. He walked out of the house and looked to the east. The sun was just beginning to show on the horizon. Above him were clouds turned a silk gray in the coming light, and he noticed how they moved quickly, as if they too felt a driving desire to be gone from this place.

Eduard walked into the house and went over to the fireplace, where he grabbed one of the thin logs from inside. He slung it across the room so that it landed just beneath the window. He watched just long enough to see the flame light the curtain. Then he grabbed another smaller log; this he carried with him outside. He walked over to the field he had spent so many years working on, and he lighted the crops in several different places.

He did not stay long enough to watch the field catch aflame, nor did he watch the house become consumed in fire. Black smoke would blanket the sky above the area, Eduard knew, but he would not see it; instead, he kept his eyes directed ahead of him. He hoped in some way that Loise and his father would understand, though he did not expect that they would.

By the time Eduard reached the village, the sun was already high up. The train to Berlin left the station at noon. The only thing he knew for sure was that he would be on that train, and once he reached Berlin he would join the *Wehrmacht.* Maybe in doing that he could be able to forget the pain in the memories.

Outings

Anais began to regularly join Eduard on his evening trips to check the traps.

The two of them would walk slowly side by side through the forest, their shadows stretching thin to the west, out to the ends of the earth, it seemed—past those places they both found comfort and safety within. At times, one of them would break the silence that hung like a calm fog between them, but it was usually some statement about the trees or a coming storm. Eduard would occasionally stop on their walks, and Anais would stand beside him while they looked out at the orange and red paintings of the sunset. They'd stay like this, their arms nearly touching, though never quite, and wait until the warmth of the colors disappeared and were replaced by the cool purples and blues of night and the stars above.

The old man grew more and more quiet as time passed. No longer did Eduard or Anais hear him humming one of the ancient tunes he often hummed. Instead, there was a calmness within the old man that had not been there before. A contentment, if such a thing could exist within a place like theirs.

When he and Anais came back from checking the traps, Eduard would hand the evening's find to the old man, who would take it and work at the animals with the knife, stripping the small things of their fur and skin. Then the three of them would sit around the flames and cook their meat.

Nights around the fire, Eduard often caught sight of the old man smiling in some unspoken thought at either he or Anais.

One night, as they sat picking at the bones of a rabbit, the old man stopped eating and held his hand up to Anais as if to quiet her. Though his hand shook gently with age, there was no other movement from the old man for several seconds. When she saw his hand, Anais set her food down and looked at him. She smiled gently at him.

The old man lowered his hand to his lap and looked at it, as if intently studying some fortune's script written on his palm. When he looked up, Anais could see that his face had changed. Instead of the calm that had become part of his features, etched into the lines of his cheeks and forehead, there was now a sort pain and anguish.

Eduard watched him quietly. He, too, noticed the change that seemed to come over the old man's face.

After several seconds of this, the old man opened his mouth and spoke, not his language, but theirs, in a voice that sounded ancient and worn. A voice that seemed to have been carried from the depths of the cave, from where the water trickled and paintings covered the walls. "Who are you?" he said.

The three of them sat looking at one another, and then, even slower this time, the old man asked again.

Anais looked over to Eduard; he was looking at her with a sense of quiet wonder at the question. She closed her eyes and nodded her head several times. Then she opened her eyes, tears beginning to run down her cheeks, and told them her story.

The Cottage

She grew up in a small village nestled along the eastern shore of the Rhine River in southern Germany. She lived there with her parents and her sister, Rachel. They lived a quiet, simple existence. In the mornings, she and her sister would wake early and collect eggs from the hens, milk the cow, and feed the other animals.

Her father worked with leather, and men would come from surrounding villages for his services; they'd bring him the hides of different animals they had killed, and he would fashion the skin into saddles or belts, sometimes shoes. He was a wide-shouldered man, and his face was covered in a thick beard that stretched down nearly to his chest. When they were little girls, Anais and Rachel would sit on their father's lap while he read tales of fairies and princesses and they'd comb their pudgy little fingers through his beard.

In 1940 Anais was seventeen years old and Rachel was fifteen. By summer that year, Germany was becoming more and more dangerous. Men brought gossip from as far away as Stuttgart and Munich, speaking of the *Reich* and of war for the country. For several months, their father kept these rumors quiet from the family, but eventually their mother overheard one of the men speaking to her husband.

It was their mother who decided they would flee from Germany and move back to France, her home country. "We cannot leave this place," their father said one evening as they sat around the table eating their meal. "They'll kill us if they find us leaving."

But their mother simply shook her head. "Then they cannot find us, Henri. We save our daughters, whatever we must do." And then she stood and walked away to begin packing clothes into one of the bags they would take.

The four of them crossed the river in the early parts of the morning and made their way into the neighboring country. After several days' journey through the forests of northern France, they came to a small stream.

Tucked away a distance into the trees, just visible from where they stood, was a small cottage. It looked to have been built a century earlier. Anais's father walked slowly over to the cottage to ask the owner for shelter and food.

After he knocked at the door for a minute, he eased it open and walked inside. It was clear that no one had lived there for a long time.

He called his family over, and together they explored the deserted cottage. Inside was a bed made of wood. A small wooden table missing a leg leaned against the wall in the corner, and there was a small stove on the other side of the cottage. Everything was covered in a thick layer of dust that floated all about them in the thin morning light that poured through a single glass window along the back wall of the place.

"This will do," their father said. "For now."

Anais and her mother and sister spent the next several days cleaning the dust from inside the cottage. Her father travelled back to Germany, back to their old home to collect additional clothing and other necessities. He brought with him several rifles his own father had given him and a pistol he had been given two years earlier.

By the time he arrived back at the cottage, he found a place hardly resembling the ruin he'd left days before. The three women took him around the surrounding areas. Berry plants were scattered all about, and they collected berries and ate them, laughing as the dark juice streamed down their chins.

"This is home now," Anais heard her mother whisper to her father one evening a month or so after they arrived, and she agreed as she closed her eyes to sleep.

They lived this quiet life for over two years.

Every few weeks, Henri left for seven or eight days and made his way across the border, back into Germany. There, he traded furs and other valuables in exchange for food and other supplies. He also gathered news of the war, and he took these things back with him through the forest.

When Rachel and Anais saw their father in his return, they would cry out across the quiet land, and he would wave to them and smile, holding up whatever new bundle he'd received. The two girls would run through the trees and embrace him, and they would walk with him over to the cottage. Once they reached the door, Anais would wait outside with Rachel and the two of them would watch as their parents embraced and kissed each other. As time passed, there would often be tears in their parents' eyes as they held each other and whispered back and forth, but Anais never asked them why. What could they be so fearful of?

It was the middle of the night when Anais woke to the sound of pounding at the door. When she sat up, Anais saw that Rachel was already awake. In the darkness of the room, Anais could see her father loading the rifles. Her mother was sitting on the edge of the bed, holding a pistol out at arm's length, pointing it with a shaking hand at the door. The pounding came again and seemed to vibrate the entire cottage. Above her, through the solitary window, a hazy glow lit the outside, as if someone had lit a match in the darkness out there. Then it moved away and all that was left was the black sky. She could hear muffled voices coming from the outside. Beside her, Rachel was sobbing and shaking, and Anais reached over and held her sister close to her.

Then the front door exploded inward. All around them, louder than anything she had ever heard, came the sound of gunfire. Anais and Rachel scrambled themselves across the floor and into the far corner, where they watched as their mother stood from where she'd been sitting, shooting the pistol at the intruders before her body twisted quickly and she fell to the ground. Rachel screamed out as she looked at her mother laying there. Across the room, farther yet, their father shot his rifle twice before he jolted backward, dropping the gun as he did so, and fell to the floor, too.

Anais closed her eyes and covered her ears with her palms, waiting for the next shot to sound. But the cottage was silent. Through her closed lids, she saw the glow of light, and she knew that someone else was in the room with them.

When she opened her eyes, she saw two men standing before her. One held a lantern high in the air so that light spilled across the small room. They wore gray uniforms and had black boots on. They looked to be ten years older than she and her sister.

"Up," one of them said in German, and gestured with his hand for them to stand. He had his pistol aimed at Anais. Neither she nor Rachel moved. He repeated the command again, more forcefully. "Up." This time, both Anais and Rachel stood. "Come here," one of the men said, and then they led the two women outside. Anais turned away from the body of her mother as they passed by. Her legs and arms were shaking, and she could hardly breathe.

Outside was another man dressed the same as the two from inside. Rachel and Anais stood in front of him, their eyes looking down, afraid of what they might see if they brought their gaze up at all.

One of the men asked the two of them questions: Where were they from? Why were they there? Why did their parents fire on members of the *Reich*?

Rachel remained quiet, and Anais stuttered answers the best she could, but she did not know how to answer the last question. The man repeated his question. Beside her, Rachel choked on a sob. One of the men, whom Anais didn't see, slapped his hand across Rachel's face hard, causing her to spin and almost fall to the ground. The man repeated the question a third time, but Anais had no answer, and so she remained quiet.

She was still looking at the ground through tears that clouded her vision, when she felt the man grab her hair and pull her head back so that she had to look directly at his face. He was a white haired man, looking much older than her father. He repeated his question again. "I don't know," Anais said finally, her lips trembling as she did so. From his side, the man took out a knife and brought it in front of her eyes. Then he cut into the left side of her face. She screamed out and tried to pull free as he moved the blade down her cheek and then up toward her ear, but the man held her hair tightly and she could not move away.

When he let go of her, she collapsed to the ground, holding her hand to her face and feeling the warm blood on her fingers. Rachel wrapped her arms around Anais, and the two of them held each other tightly, as if their embrace could ward off whatever evil it was that surrounded them.

Rachel and Anais stayed the night outside. The men in uniforms had tied them with rope, and the two of them could only sit up. The entire night, Anais worked at the rope with her hands, but she couldn't get the tight knots loosened. By morning, she had given up and, instead, sat there, whispering words of hope to Rachel, who sat against the wall of the cottage, silently looking out at the grove of trees a distance off.

Anais told her sister that they would escape. "Somehow we will," she said. Rachel nodded her head slightly, but Anais was unsure if her sister had actually heard.

By late morning, the three men were awake. Conversation came from inside, and a little while later, one of the younger men walked out to them. He was eating a handful of berries that Rachel and Anais had picked with their mother the day before.

Without a word, the man reached down and dragged Rachel inside. The door shut loudly behind them. After several seconds, Anais heard Rachel's screams, and she began to cry as she sat there listening to her sister, knowing that there was nothing she could do to stop the pain and hurt. She worked at the knots again, this time feverishly, digging the heels of her bare feet into the dirt, as if she were trying to push herself through the wall and into the cottage. Her body shook as she listened to Rachel.

After several minutes, Rachel's screams stopped, and the door opened and Rachel, sobbing, was led outside by the two younger men. She was told to sit down beside her sister. Rachel had been untied from the ropes, and when she sat, she looked over at Anais with vacant eyes, red and wet from the screams. It no longer looked to be Rachel, but some other creature inhabiting the woman's face.

The white-haired man came out and grabbed at Anais and took her inside. Before the man shut the door, he told the other two to stay outside.

Inside the cottage, the man brought Anais over to the bed and sat her down. He looked at the man. At his hip, attached to his belt was his knife, the one used to cut her face the night previous. He sat down beside her and began to undo the ropes. Once she was untied, he directed her to lie down. As he was positioning himself over her, Anais closed her eyes and, with all her might, brought both of her hands up at the man's throat. The blow made him fall back, and he tried to scream, but he was unable to. He clutched at his throat and neck, and while he lay there, twisting in pain, Anais moved quickly over to her mother's body and picked up the gun that was resting beside her mother's head. Anais had never held a gun before, and it was heavier than she thought.

She walked over to where the man was and, from a distance of several steps, she raised the gun at his head and pulled the trigger. His head jolted back hard. Behind him, the wall and ground was covered in a spray of blood, and blood pooled from under his head and spread out around him. Her legs shook beneath her, and she would have fallen down if the door had not burst open just then. She turned quickly, raising the gun as she did so. When the first man came through the door, she fired the pistol again and watched as a space on his cheek erupted into a gaping hole. He fell forward into the cottage, dead. The other man came to the door; he was reaching at his hip to remove his own pistol. She fired again, but missed his head, hitting his shoulder instead. He turned and screamed out, falling down outside the cottage.

Anais dropped the gun. Her heart was beating hard inside her chest. She looked over and saw her mother's coat on top of the table and grabbed it before she quickly ran out the door, stepping over the dead man and then past the other man she had just shot. He was still screaming and holding his shoulder while he lay on the ground, kicking his feet hard into the dirt. She moved over to where Rachel sat and pulled her sister to her feet. "Go," she screamed, and the two of them ran away from the cottage, unsure of where they were heading.

Rachel ran staggering beside her, and Anais looked over to tell her that things would be okay, that she would be safe, but just as she did, Anais heard the gunshot and then saw her sister's body fall forward. Behind her, the man had gotten to his feet and was holding a pistol out in front of him. More gunshots sounded, and tree bark and branches exploded all around Anais. She reached down to pull Rachel to her feet again, but saw the blood trickling from out her sister's mouth and Anais knew she was alone.

The gunshots stopped, and when she looked back at him,

Anais saw that he was trying to load another magazine into the pistol, but was having difficulty doing so with his injured shoulder.

By the time he finished and looked up to see where she was, Anais had disappeared, becoming a ghost among the trees.

Like Wind

Outside the cave, the summer sun was beginning its descent. What light that came in from the opening would soon disappear completely. Anais was just rising from where she sat, the book of Shakespeare still in her hand, when they heard the first explosions. Below them, the stone floor seemed to vibrate, as if a train were travelling nearby.

With the first explosion, the three of them fell to the ground and covered their heads, even the old man, who had been walking toward the entrance to go relieve himself outside. Small rocks broke loose from the cave ceiling and walls and fell around them. Anais thought she could hear the sound of the cave ripping in two, but when she looked up, she saw that the dark walls were still intact. Then came another explosion, and then a series of several more—too many to count.

After several minutes, the explosions stopped, and Eduard stood and walked quickly to the entrance of the cave and then outside. Anais watched him from where she knelt, willing herself to stand and follow after him. There was a strange silence and calm that came then, and during those minutes Anais could hear the beat of her heart and feel her temples throbbing. The rock beneath her knees cut into her skin, and she tried to adjust herself, but it did not help the pain and so she remained where she was. It wasn't until the explosions began again that she pushed herself up from the floor of the cave and ran toward the entrance. There had been something more terrifying about the silence than there was with the sounds of explosions. As she was about to walk outside, she looked back at the old man and saw that he was now sitting up. There was a look of peace on his face, and he lifted his hand in greeting or parting, she couldn't tell which. Anais returned the gesture and then went outside.

Eduard was sitting on a bed of dirt and pine needles several steps away from her. The horizon was turning a navy-black color, and the stars had begun to blanket the sky.

Anais walked over and sat beside Eduard. From where they were, she could not tell from which direction the explosions were coming. The bursts seemed to surround the two of them sitting there, just as the sound of their laughter echoed from off the walls within the cave.

They could not tell how long they stayed out there, sitting quietly beside each other. Like so many other things, time had become an irrelevant aspect of life in the cave. What use was there counting time or keeping track of the moments within a life that none of them knew for a fact they were living.

The explosions continued to come in intermittent patterns, stops and starts. Single bursts and then too many to tell apart.

"It's a distance away still," Eduard said to her, and she nodded, not knowing how else to respond. And though they could not see any effect of the noise, no bursts of light out there in the dark, they kept their eyes trained on the distant horizon, barely noticing the trees as they disappeared into the black of night.

"What do you think the end of the world will sound like?" she asked him.

"Like that, I think," he said, and the two of them listened to the constant eruption of noise around them.

Neither moved.

Then the explosions stopped completely, and the forest and all of its surroundings was quiet once again.

"Is it over?" Anais asked.

Eduard was silent for several seconds before he answered. "For now," he said.

Their backs were rigid as they waited for sounds that may or may not come again. In the silence, Anais set her hand down on the ground beside her and moved it gently back and forth. She felt the dry texture of the dust and the dirt, the sharp prick of pine needles on her fingertips. The tiny pebbles that rolled under her palm. Silence. Peace in this moment. Then, slowly, she stretched her hand out over the ground, inching her fingers toward Eduard until she felt the skin of his hand. He moved his hand away quickly, but then put it back where it had been, allowing her fingers to move over his, as if she were trying to read a hidden message on his skin: words invisible to the eye. She let her hand come to rest covering his. After several seconds, he turned his hand over so that their palms came together, and he wrapped his fingers gently around hers.

Neither Eduard nor Anais looked down at where their hands connected; neither looked over at the other. Instead, they simply kept their gaze ahead.

He was the first to speak and break the silence that had settled between them. "What will you do after?" he asked. His voice was calmer than she'd ever heard it before. Quiet, as if he was afraid to speak loudly and disrupt this moment.

Anais dropped her head down a bit, so that she could see her knees as well as the dark earth that seemed to stretch out beyond her imagining. Then she looked over at him. "After what?"

"After this is all over." He looked at her.

She sighed and then turned her head away again, letting her eyes settle back on the forest. "Will there ever be an after? Or will this be all we know?"

He nodded. "I thought I would stay here forever. Grow old and die in the cave."

"But that's not living," she said.

"No. I guess it isn't. But what is living?"

"I don't know."

"Neither do I. But I miss it."

They let a silence settle between them. Their hands still held on to one another. During the time they sat there, crickets played their songs. Above, squirrels scampered about. Anais looked up and wondered at the bugs and small animals around them, wondering if they had been silent while the explosions shattered the distant sky, or had those things' lives simply carried on while she had chosen not to hear.

She looked back over at Eduard. He was gently biting at his lower lip, and she smiled at how he sat, though she did not know why. "What will you do, then? After."

"When I was young, my father took me once to the ocean in the west of Germany. It took days to get there on the train, but when we got there, I remember I had never seen anything so beautiful. I remember thinking that I could stay there my entire life and I would be happy. I walked out into the water. It was so cold—I still dream of the water, of walking out into it, and the sounds of the birds that were everywhere. My father was happier than I had ever seen him. For the only time in my life, the world seemed perfect." He was silent for several seconds, and he bit at his lower lip some more, as if he were trying to accept the reality of this memory. Anais could feel his fingers gently twitch within her hold. "There was a lighthouse there; it was painted red and white. It was so tall, I remember." He nodded his head. "I would like to sit and watch its light shine out onto the ocean again. That's where I would go."

She smiled and felt a strange peace, as if in his telling she had become part of the memory. As if she were seeing the world through his eyes.

Gently, almost without his realizing, Anais squeezed Eduard's hand a little more tightly, and he smiled, feeling happiness for the first time in years.

When they returned to the cave, the fire inside had almost burned itself out. Even though the air was warm, Eduard added two more logs, and, within a minute, the small area was brightly lit.

The old man was not there. When Anais asked, Eduard told her that he was probably out in the woods and that he would be back soon. The old man had still not returned by the time the two of them were readying themselves for sleep. When he was not there in the morning, Eduard realized that the old man was not coming back, wherever he was. He knew that the old man had simply disappeared, like some benevolent spirit of the forest, and that Eduard would never be able to thank him for the quiet friendship they shared.

Soldiers

They came several days later, after the old man disappeared.

Eduard had just returned from walking the depths of the cave when he heard voices coming from outside the entrance. Anais was asleep, leaning against the side wall of the cave where the old man used to sit. Held loosely in her hand still was the book of Shakespeare that she had been reading again and again since she first finished it.

Eduard walked over and touched her shoulder.

When she opened her eyes, she saw Eduard standing over her, a finger to his lips. His body blocked out the thin streak of sunlight from the entrance.

"Go," he whispered.

Anais stood quickly. "Where?"

Eduard looked around the cave, as if searching for some hidden room he'd once known of long ago but had simply forgotten. Then he brought his attention back to Anais. From his pocket, he pulled out the lighter and handed it to her. "Go in as far as you can," he said. "Past the paintings. Don't stop."

"I can't," she said. Tears formed at the corners of her eyes.

He brought his hands up to her face, resting them gently on her cheeks, and wiped the tears away with his thumbs. Even in the dark, Eduard could see that her lips were trembling. She shook her head. "Stop it," he said. He brought his hands away from her face and then grabbed her wrist and placed the lighter in her hand. He closed her fingers around it. "Don't use it unless you need to."

Anais nodded her head. "I'm sorry," she whispered and then turned and began walking into the darkness of the cave.

Eduard watched until he could see her no more, until she became one more thing hidden in the darkness. Then he moved: first over to where the supplies lay against the side wall, where he picked up one of the pistols that had sat there untouched for years, and then toward the entrance. He turned and looked over the strange place that had become his home. It was dark. The fire was nearly extinguished, and the faint smell of smoke and burned meat seemed to float throughout the air. He reached out and placed an open hand on the wall, feeling with it all the memories—the joys and pains, fears and hopes—that had become tattooed there.

At the entrance, he gripped the pistol tightly in his hand. His palm was sweating. Outside, he could see six men in the brown colors of the French army. They had rifles slung across their backs; two of them were looking at a map, while another was drinking from a canteen, and the other three were huddled about together, talking with smiles on their faces. Eduard could not tell what they were saying to each other.

They were twenty or so steps away, and he wondered if they might not even come to find the cave, but there was too much risk in waiting. He thought of Anais walking deep into the places of the cave that only he knew of, and he smiled at the image of her dragging her fingers along the side wall as he told her all those months before. He thought of the old man, hoping wherever he was that he was safe.

Then, without any more thought or regret, without fear or even hope, Eduard took a deep breath and ran outside, firing shots from the pistol into the air while he ran away from the soldiers and away from the entrance of the cave.

When she heard the explosions of gunfire, Anais stopped walking and turned back in the direction she had come. She wanted to call out, to scream for him, to bring him back to her, though she could not. Instead, she let herself fall slowly to the ground, where she stayed for a long while, crying tears that fell from her face and disappeared within the darkness that surrounded her.

Waiting

All he could see when he opened his eyes were blurry figures in white and gray, and darkness behind them. The colorless forms seemed to glide back and forth slowly, and though he tried to follow them with his eyes, he could not. When he tried to raise his hands to rub at his eyes with his palms, Eduard realized that his arms had been bound with straps and that he could hardly move. He tried to sit up, but a sharp pain in his left leg and the side of his abdomen forced him to give up the effort and lay his head back down on the hard cot he had been sleeping on. He screamed out in pain and frustration and then tried to sit up again. This time, though, he felt hands grab hold of his shoulders and push him forcefully into the cot.

"*Ne pas*," a man's voice said, but Eduard could not see anything but blotchy shapes still. He screamed out and pushed with his shoulders against the hands, against the restraints on his arms, against the vague images that surrounded him, but he was unable to move even the slightest. "*Ne pas*," the voice said again. He could not understand the language, and his body shook from the pain and from the fear. Then, from the clouded world, he saw another white figure move above him and place a cloth over his face. And then everything went black and he felt nothing more.

He woke again several hours later.

Pillows had been placed behind his back and behind his head to prop him up so that he was sitting. He could move his arms now, and he lifted his hands to his face, rubbing his nose and his closed eyes. He felt a slight throbbing from his leg and his side, but it was nothing like the pain he had felt when last he'd been awake. He opened his eyes again, realizing that this time he could see the world clearly.

The large, open room was lit in a dull light, though he could not tell from where exactly the light was coming. It reminded him of mornings back on the farm, just as the sun was rising and light was beginning to show over the eastern horizon, when the day was full of possibilities and hope. Directly across from him, several steps away, was a man lying on a cot. Beside the man was another cot, and beside him was another and another. Eduard's eyes moved along the row of cots. Most were occupied with men, many of whom were sleeping beneath thin blankets, their heads or arms wrapped in white bandages that seemed to glow in the minimal lighting of the place. Above him, Eduard noticed the fabric of the ceiling, and he followed it down, along the wall on which the head of his own cot rested. He was in a hospital tent, he realized. To his left, he could see more cots, though most of these were empty. In that direction was the flap of the tent, beyond which he saw the bright sunlight of the outside world.

"Hello," a voice said from his right. Though the voice was German, Eduard could hear the accent in it. It sounded like Anais's accent.

When he turned to his right, Eduard saw two men sitting in chairs. A woman dressed in white, a nurse, stood near the foot of the bed. Her head was covered by a white cap, and in her hand she held a towel.

The first of the men, the one closest to Eduard, sat erect. He wore a thin mustache, and his black hair was slicked back and it seemed to shine in the muted light. Eduard could tell from the man's uniform that he was a French captain. The man sitting beside the captain, near Eduard's legs, also wore the colors of France, but his dress showed that he was merely a soldier; this man sat slumped forward, his elbows resting on his knees.

The first man said something, but Eduard could not understand, and he shook his head at the speech. The man repeated, but again Eduard shook his head. Then the second man spoke. Eduard recognized this man's voice as the one who had spoken the greeting only a moment earlier. "He says, 'Where do you come from?'"

Eduard tried to sit up taller, but he felt a pain shoot through his left leg and he grimaced. "What happened?" he asked.

The second man spoke to the first in French, and the first answered back. Eduard watched the exchange carefully, trying to understand what was being said between the men.

"You don't remember?" the second man asked.

Eduard shook his head.

"What do you remember?"

Eduard took a deep breath and then released it slowly. "I ran out . . ." he trailed off.

"And then?"

The first man leaned forward, toward Eduard, and then settled himself back in his chair. Eduard shook his head. "Nothing else."

The first man spoke again in French. The second translated. "Why did you shoot at French soldiers?"

Eduard's hands shook, and he clenched his fists, trying to keep them still. He looked away, toward the entrance of the tent, and then again at the two men sitting before him. The colors of their clothing, the first man's mustache, the way it seemed to twitch slightly. "I thought they were German. *Wehrmacht.* And I didn't shoot at them. Only in the sky, to scare them."

The two men spoke in French, the second gesturing at times toward him, and then he turned back to Eduard. "You remember that? Though you said you remembered nothing else."

"Nothing after that. I remember running and then nothing until I woke here."

His words were translated; then the second turned to Eduard again. "You were shot once in the leg, just above your knee, and once in your abdomen, though it missed your stomach and chest. Neither are serious."

Eduard nodded.

"You hit your head when you fell and lost consciousness. You have medication to help with the pain now. But that is only now. That can change, if . . ." The second man's voice trailed off.

"If what?"

"If you do not answer our questions. Tell us who you are."

Eduard looked over to the nurse, but she turned away, looking, instead, at one of the beds a short distance off. He looked back to the second man. "What do you want? I'll tell you."

Over the next hour, Eduard fashioned a fiction of his life, a fiction he so desperately wished was true.

Every minute or so, the second man raised a hand to stop Eduard while he translated to the captain what was said.

Eduard began by telling them that his name was Wilbert Meyer, his father's name. "I was not in the *Wehrmacht*, though I was supposed to be," he said.

He told them of how he had been a farmer, like his father and his father's father. "I was told to join, but I couldn't. The day before I was to leave for Berlin, I left." It took him weeks to walk into France, he said. He travelled only during the night, for fear of being found by German soldiers.

He walked until he came upon a cave, and he entered inside, nearing starvation, only to find an old man, who took care of him, nursed him back to health. It was the old man, Eduard told them, who had collected the materials in the cave. "Everything was there when I arrived. Even clothing. That's why I was dressed as I was."

When asked about the old man, Eduard only said that the man did not speak German and that the old man was the only human he had seen or spoken with during those years. "No one else," Eduard said, shaking his head. As he did so, he thought of Anais and wondered whether she had gotten away.

When the second man said that no one else had been found in the cave, Eduard smiled quietly, though the men did not understand why. The second man asked where the old man was, and Eduard could only answer with the truth: "He left," he said. "One evening, I came back to the cave and he was gone."

Eduard finished his story, telling of the French soldiers outside the cave. "I'm sorry," he said to them. "I thought they were German. They would have killed me if they were German. I'm a traitor to them. I would have rather tried to escape than be found in the cave alone."

After the second man translated these words, the captain nodded and then stood up. He was followed behind by the second of the two, and they walked off toward the opening of the tent, neither of them speaking, neither looking at any of the wounded men they passed by.

The nurse, who had been standing the whole time, walked over and eased Eduard down, taking the pillows from his back, so that he was lying again. Then she dipped the towel into a bowl of water and began to wipe at Eduard's sweaty forehead and neck.

He drifted off to sleep while she did this, the whole while thinking of Anais and how he had done the same for her. It seemed a separate life now; one he wished to return to.

He stayed in the hospital tent for several weeks. During that time, he did not see either of the two men who had questioned him. Instead, each day, one of the six nurses there took care of him, feeding him soup and meat, bread, occasionally. They washed his face and arms and legs, his stomach and back. They gently turned him every few hours to keep sores from forming. Every morning and afternoon he sat up and watched the goings on of the place.

There was so much pain surrounding him, and he found himself often wondering at the purpose of life. Was the world simply constructed of hurt and sadness and bloodshed? Was each person born into this world crying for the lost innocence that he could never have again?

He often saw nurses rush to one of the cots. They'd surround the man lying there, screaming orders to one another. Many times, they stayed there for several minutes until they all walked slowly away from the cot, their heads hanging low, blood, sometimes, on their hands and arms and clothing. Two or three soldiers would come minutes later and take the body away.

Eduard's wounds were not bad. The bullet had grazed his side, and the gunshot to his leg, though painful, had missed all bone and had ripped minimal muscle. He would walk with a heavy limp the rest of his life, but he was able to recover quickly.

After the fifth week, the nurses began to teach him to walk with the aid of crutches. A week later, they led him out of the tent and into the blinding sunlight. The nurses beside him smiled as he made his way around the small area outside the tent. He looked around him and saw that he was still somewhere in the forest, though he did not know exactly where.

During those weeks, Eduard often thought of Anais. He struggled to recall her face, remembering instead her voice within the darkness of the cave. He found his thoughts returning again and again to the night when they had held hands as they sat and listened to the thundering drums of the bombs. Her hand on his, feeling so light, like air moving over wet skin. That moment became part of him over those weeks, a history written on his palms. When he woke from the memory, Eduard would hold his hand up to his face, searching for some indication that the dream had been real, but there was nothing.

At night, he would lie awake on his cot and stare into the darkness above him. Shadowed hillsides formed on the fabric ceiling and horses ran along the seams of the tent while birds flew over their heads. Wheat and barley moved like liquid around the shadow animals, and he smiled at this, remembering the world as it once was. When he closed his eyes, the horses from the tent ceiling would turn into obscure beasts whose names were too ancient to pronounce. In these dream-thoughts, the beasts moved slowly around him—creatures that only existed as memories painted on a cave wall, hidden from the world. As they moved off into the darkness of his mind, he wondered if he, too, would disappear, or would anyone remember the words he spoke, the life he lived?

One morning seven and a half weeks after he found himself in the hospital tent, Eduard woke to one of the nurses sitting in a chair beside his cot. He sat up and looked at her.

She smiled, though she did not speak—he wouldn't have understood what she was saying if she had spoken. Instead, she simply pointed off in the direction of the tent's opening. Eduard followed the direction with his eyes, noticing that he was one of the last men still there; the others had either died or been taken away, many of them back to Paris or to their hometowns. Back to their lives.

Then Eduard looked back to the nurse. She nodded quietly and Eduard knew what she was there to tell him: he was able to leave the hospital tent and journey out into the world again.

He smiled back to her and nodded his head. Then he moved his legs so that they hung over the side of the cot and, with the help of the nurse, reached for the crutches.

The After

Eduard was driven to a nearby city by two French soldiers. He sat in the back of the vehicle, keeping his head down, afraid to look at either of the men, afraid they might see through the lies he had told, but neither of them paid him any attention.

At the city, the two soldiers helped him down from the vehicle and walked him up the stairs of the station. He was to board the first train heading north, toward the German border. There, he would be directed further as to where to go.

Eduard sat on one of the vacant benches and watched as the two soldiers walked away; they were smiling and laughing to each other, and Eduard felt a strange envy he had not felt in a long time. He looked around him, seeing men and women move about the streets of the city on their normal daily routines, as if they had nothing to fear. As if there had not just been violence and war and bloodshed all around them.

Above him, the sky was a deep blue, and he watched as a cloud moved across the sky.

Eduard remembered seeing the city's name on a map he found in one of the dead men's packs. He used to study the map in the darkness of the cave, wondering what life must be like in any one of the many villages named on the paper.

As he sat on the bench, Eduard closed his eyes and listened to the wind pass by. It would take him a long time, he knew, but he needed to go, and so he stood up and slowly made his way out of the city.

By the time the train pulled into the station, Eduard had been gone for half an hour.

It took him a little over a week to come to the clearing in the forest. For those days, Eduard lived on berries and whatever other food he could find. When he was tired, he stopped and slept. He drank from the streams, feeling the cold of the water on his lips and his cheeks. There was a peace in the surroundings, as if the trees guided him, comforting and sheltering him along his journey back.

Eduard passed through the clearing slowly. The ground felt soft under his feet, and as he walked he spoke words of apologies to the men who were buried all around him.

From the clearing, he walked the familiar path back to the cave.

It was late morning when he saw the entrance. He quickened his pace a little, letting the worn and splintered feet of the crutches scrape noisily over the pine needles and rocks.

He felt like crying when he bent down and entered the cave. It was dark inside, save for the thin streak of sunlight that spilled onto the stone floor. Though it had only been weeks, the place looked different than he remembered it. No longer did it hold the warmth he came to know there. The fire had burned out long ago and now there was only scattered ash.

Eduard walked over to the side wall where the supplies had been—the coats and weapons, books and blankets—but those things were gone now. The cave stretched beyond him in total darkness. He wanted to call out, cry out her name, though he did not. Instead, he turned back to the entrance, feeling the breeze from deep within the cave blow gently around him.

He was about to walk out into the sunlight when he stopped and turned back for one last look at the place he called home for so many years. He looked over to the side of the cave, to where he had brought her.

Eduard slowly walked over and knelt down. His leg hurt, and he needed to put his hand down to catch himself from falling. He remembered kneeling in this same spot, watching over her while she slept, bathing her with the wet cloth. He took a deep breath.

As he was about to stand, he saw a small object sitting on the ground in front of him. He picked it up and nearly dropped it once he realized what he held. It was the lighter he had given her all those weeks ago. Tears formed in his eyes and he smiled. Knowing.

He flicked at the lighter several times, watching the sparks come and then vanish in the darkness. He flicked it once more and watched as a flame appeared. Then he looked up and saw it.

Covering the smoke-stained wall was a drawing in white chalk: the image of a lighthouse. Surrounding its base were waves, and a short distance off were two figures, one a man with a beard and the other a woman with hair that stretched down her back. They were holding hands.

Beneath the two figures were words written out in a shaky script, and Eduard needed to wipe away the tears in order to read them. He brought the flame closer to the wall and then spoke the words aloud, smiling.

"Come find me in the after."

Brandon Daily is the author of two novels, *A Murder Country* and *The Valley*. His short fiction, nonfiction, plays, and poetry have appeared in numerous journals and magazines. He currently lives in Southern California with his wife and two children.

Made in the USA
Columbia, SC
04 December 2019

84326373R00138